## UNDER THE STARS

When they started shivering, they got up and lit the Coleman lantern, pitched Kip's new tent, and got inside.

"It's too cold to get naked," she said. Her teeth chattered.

"Where there's a will, there's a way," he muttered as he twisted open the button on the waistband of her jeans and tugged the zipper down.

He kissed her, and she relaxed a little. They knelt on the sleeping bag and pretty soon she realized he was right—there was a way.

She saw: his bony face, grinning. His dark hair falling in his eyes. She touched: his navel, his dimple, his skinny ribs. She breathed: coffee, lust, soap, cold. His breath in time with hers, warm and damp, then she was gone, falling off the mountain. And never hit bottom.

Also by Lenore Carroll

*Love with a Warm Cowboy*

Available from
HarperPaperbacks

# The Heart Remembers

*Lenore Carroll*

HarperPaperbacks
*A Division of* HarperCollins*Publishers*

This is a work of fiction. The characters, incidents, and dialogues are products of the author's imagination and are not to be construed as real. Any resemblance to actual events or persons, living or dead, is entirely coincidental.

HarperPaperbacks *A Division of* HarperCollins*Publishers*
10 East 53rd Street, New York, N.Y. 10022



Cover photography by Herman Estevez

First printing: December 1993

Printed in the United States of America



❖ 10 9 8 7 6 5 4 3 2 1

*To Gloria Briggs and Ray Puechner.*
*They always said I could do it.*

## ACKNOWLEDGMENTS

My sincere thanks to Pamela B. Daddow and Bill Eppridge, without whose help I could not have written this novel. If the story is believable, it is thanks to them. Any errors are mine. I also gratefully acknowledge the help of John Lofflin, Ron Miriani, Ann Schultis, Sarah Morgan, Win Blevins, and John Mort.

# 1

*Kip escaped blowing snow* and air too cold to breathe when he walked into the lobby of the old Valverde Hotel in Socorro, New Mexico on this last day of 1964. A blizzard white and cold as the old year marked its close.

Most of his cameras were safely snugged into their plush-lined cases, but Kip kept taking pictures in his head. One Leica hung inside his coat, accessible, its weight potent against his ribs.

He looked at the room with a photographer's eye—a gray room, lighted with kerosene lamps, an old L-shaped hotel desk beyond the pillars. Clusters of people, refugees from the snow, in sheepskin coats, old wool topcoats, hats still on heads, gloves still on hands. F 1.4, Kip decided, if their faces were close enough to the light. Hell, Tri-X at 1000 ASA. Might be enough. Worth a try. He brought the camera to his eye.

Light entered the tall, narrow windows from the streetlamp out back, filtered through horizontal snow, not enough light, not enough.

One couple—young, still ruddy from the cold—argued in rattling Spanish near a potbellied stove that smoked as if it hadn't been used since the Coolidge administration. She was pregnant, and her husband was angry. If only Kip had a couple of flashlights. The woman had a beautiful Indian face and long hair. He jammed his elbows into his ribs for a fifteenth of a second. If only everyone would hold still and quit breathing.

The people in the hotel lobby, mostly couples and families, reminded Kip of photographs of people in London subways during the Blitz. Raised on *Life* magazine pictures, he saw the world in black and white on an 10" x 13" page, with the red logo on the cover.

There was a pretty girl, light falling on her cheek. That might work. Irish face, no makeup and no teased hair. No heavy eyeliner, no frosted eyelids, no false eyelashes. Natural, lovely. Why was she traveling alone? Unheard of. Where was she headed on New Year's Eve?

He looked through the camera at a man in a worn sheepskin jacket. Too dark even for the rangefinder? You could go cross-eyed trying to align the images in this light. It was like looking through fog.

Kip walked over to the stove. It was perhaps eight degrees warmer closer to the black iron. He looked up, but it was too dark to see why it smoked, what was wrong with the galvanized pipe that angled across the ceiling to a window. One pane had been replaced with wood and a metal collar for the pipe.

The state police had stopped Kip's car halfway between El Paso and Albuquerque. He couldn't have gone on anyway. Traffic had been directed off Interstate 25 to this old hotel. Part of the building was used—a bookshop and offices opened off the courtyard. But the hotel part looked as though someone had begun rehabilitating the lobby and then ran out of money.

The old cord-and-plug switchboard stood on the floor in a corner, and cans of paint were stacked in a pyramid behind the desk. One wall was torn down to the laths. Valverde Hotel dated, according to a framed news clipping, from 1919. The original woodwork at the top of the pillars was perfect, and the rest awaited the paint stripper that was lined up with the paint by the desk.

Nobody seemed to be in charge as each relay of state cops ushered a carful of people inside and disappeared, presumably to shanghai another. One family bedded down children not too far from the stove, then a man in a stained apron arrived with an urn of coffee and a stack of paper cups. Kip gladly took a cup then edged away, leaned against the desk, and dropped his backpack.

The pretty girl claimed two feet of her own and sat with her back leaning against the wall. When she finished her coffee she ate a Snickers bar, then took a bath towel out of her backpack, rolled it into a backrest, and watched the commotion of people coming and going and arguing and claiming space on the wide-plank floor.

Kip was still wired from driving into the snow. Two hours gripping the wheel, not able to see anything but the white lines against the snow-swept asphalt. He had been afraid he would run into a car, or afraid a car would plow into him. Visibility: the chrome ornament at the end of his car hood.

Most of the people resigned themselves to spending the night. The young couple had stopped arguing. The husband sulked, and the wife stared out the front windows, the snow casting a lavender light on her face. Snow banked against the arches of the *portale* and at the corner where the waist-high adobe wall met the side of the building. The wrought-iron gate, its design Moorish and delicate, appeared and disappeared from view as the wind gusted through the court.

Kip looked at the girl and found her looking back. Instead of dropping her eyes demurely, or holding his gaze brazenly, she grinned and shrugged, as if to say, "Might as well make the most of it."

"Mind of I crash here?" Kip asked, standing over her.

She shrugged again. He would remember the casual way it all began, the images he mentally photographed, the cold, stuffy air in the lobby. He would remember her eyes, dancing, aware. He would remember her pink cheeks, her lips cracked from the cold.

The Indian woman's huge, scowling husband backhanded her. She cried out and fell to the floor. Kip jumped up and stepped between them. He was inches shorter and about forty pounds lighter than the husband.

"Leave her alone!" he shouted to the man.

The husband swung at Kip, who ducked, then the woman cried out again, doubled over. Her waters had broken. Kip grabbed his sleeping bag, unrolled it for her to lie on, and asked, "Can somebody help me?"

None of the people clustered around the stove replied, so Jess stepped in and held the woman through each contraction. She didn't want to get involved and she was growing tired of propping the woman up. Her back ached, and she was afraid somebody would sue her for impersonating a nurse. Why did I get into this? she thought. There were other, older women, but not one came forward.

"What's the matter, scout?" Kip asked. He looked up

from between the laboring woman's legs and grinned. Jess tried to smile back.

"I feel like I got lost in a movie of the week," she said. "Every ethnic group represented, crisis situation, the husband's the bad guy."

Jess always joked to cover up. She wanted to leave, but the woman leaned against her, and Kip looked to her for encouragement. She was scared. She only had a rough idea of what was supposed to happen. What if something went wrong? Was there a hospital in Socorro?

Irrelevant images ran through her head—scenes from old movies, her own GYN exam, the light from the lanterns, the smell of woodsmoke from the stove. She heard a couple of truckers grousing about schedules. Conversations rose and fell within families who wouldn't get back to Albuquerque, Santa Fe, Farmington, or Gallup that night. The gale winds threatened the windows.

The birth smells, rich as fresh sweat, rose from the woman. What happened next?

"Where's the cavalry to the rescue?" Kip muttered. A white line of panic grew around his mouth. The woman groaned.

"Omigod, it's coming!"

Jess had never been this close to a birth. The woman's husband waited across the lobby, seeming unconcerned. Strands of the woman's straight black hair lay plastered to her cheeks and neck. She ground her teeth and squeezed Jess's hand so hard it lost all feeling.

Why hadn't one of the older women, one with kids, jumped in? They at least would know what was happening. The state police might know. This guy, Kip, looked so young—like a boy scout, with his pocketknife on a clean handkerchief—serious, intent. His roguish grin didn't inspire confidence, but he seemed to know what he was doing. He squatted between the woman's legs in a catcher's pose, hands waiting.

Jess's heart pounded. She felt her face stretch in a huge smile she couldn't stop. She was scared and excited and curious and she didn't want to be here and she wouldn't miss it for the world. My God, it was so simple.

The woman gave a final cry, and the baby slipped out. It was a red, wrinkled baby girl, covered with blood and creamy white stuff. Jess's eyes filled with tears of relief as she stroked the woman's damp hair back from her face. The woman panted and groaned.

Kip grabbed Jess's towel and wrapped the baby in it. He looked into the little face. The baby choked and he ran his finger inside and pulled out mucus. Then the baby mewed, and the mother smiled. Kip looked to see if the baby's throat was clear, then handed the infant to her mother.

A thick, heavy smell came from Kip's bloody sleeping bag, but the baby, blotched with vernix and blood, smelled wonderful. Jess thought she'd never smelled anything so good.

"I think you have to cut the cord," Jess said. The woman nodded.

"Right!" Kip looked around. "Do you have anything?"

Jess crawled over to her backpack and pulled out a grosgrain hair ribbon.

"Cut it in two," he said, handing her his Boy Scout knife.

She divided the ribbon and gave him one piece. This was far from sterile. He struggled to tie the ribbon around the twisted, slippery umbilical cord. Then he took the other piece and tied it a few inches down. Jess held the knife blade in the flame of Kip's Zippo for thirty seconds, waited for it to cool, and then handed it to him.

He cut the cord.

Jess watched the mother, who unwrapped the baby to count fingers and toes. After a while, the afterbirth oozed out. Jess began cleaning up the woman with clean paint rags. Kip was tender and proud and bursting with energy.

Then he looked at Jess, puzzled.

"What's the matter?" she asked.

"Is this all we do?"

"I thought you'd done this before!"

"I'm a photographer. Why would I know anything about birthing babies, Miz Scarlett?"

"You acted so confident."

"I always act confident."

Panic froze Jess's lungs, and she couldn't breathe again.

The woman mumbled something in Spanish, then English.

Kip tipped the baby so more mucus could drain. After a few minutes, the baby issued a reedy wail. The mother smiled. The baby cried louder. Then Jess could breathe again, clear down to her diaphragm.

The sleeping bag was ruined, and the woman needed to be cleaned again. Did she have sanitary napkins? Did Jess?

Jess went into the ladies' room, praying that the water was on. It was, and she wrung out a towel in the icy water, held it in front of the stove to warm, and then cleaned the woman.

When she finished the husband embraced his family, wrapped his wife in his huge, grimy parka, and murmured a litany of Spanish endearments as he moved his wife and child closer to the stove.

Kip danced around with a proprietary air, warning the

other refugees to give the mother room. His camera was out. He aimed and he pushed the button. What kind of nut was he? Jess consigned the sleeping bag to a plastic garbage can filled with plaster and lumber scraps. She hadn't felt this high since her softball team had won the regional championship, since she had made Phi Beta Kappa.

She wanted to grab Kip and run through the snow, eat a dozen hamburgers.

She wanted to howl with joy.

A perfect child!

In the ladies' room, she scrubbed her hands and face hard as though high spirits could cling to her skin. If watching somebody else have a baby felt this good, what must it be like to have your own?

A pair of state troopers arrived with an electric space heater as she returned to the lobby. Kip told them what happened. Jess looked through the French doors into the dining room, wishing there was something to eat. Square pillars and painted dadoes, large tables covered with dust, and a huge wooden icebox—all looking as though they hadn't been used for years.

Kip stood in the lobby waiting for her, hands in his jeans pockets, grinning again.

"We did pretty good, partner," he said.

"For two people who didn't know what they were doing."

She grabbed him in a congratulatory hug. Kip threw his arms around her and swung her off her feet. "Thank God the mother knew what *she* was doing," he said.

Jess liked the wiry strength of his arms. "We ought to celebrate." She wanted to add to the general commotion —people explaining to the troopers, families talking, the new father hovering.

"I was going to buy food in Albuquerque," he said.

"I've got some Ritz crackers in my backpack."

Before she could get them out, people from town arrived with sandwiches and milk and soft drinks.

After they ate, they leaned on their backpacks against the wall. Clusters of people stood eating and talking around the only table, voices raised—always voices. The dark jackets of the troopers moved through the crowd.

"I thought it would be holy, like a sacrament. Or technical. Mostly it was hard work," Jess said.

"Must be why they call it labor. I kept wishing I had another set of hands so I could take pictures. Does that sound weird?"

"How could you think of pictures at a time like that?"

"I always think of pictures."

"Are you thinking of photographing now?"

He nodded and pulled the camera from under his coat, twisted the lens, shrugged. "Not enough light."

"If there was enough light, would you be taking pictures?"

"Probably. It's what I do."

Jess shook her head. "I can't believe it. You think about making pictures all the time?"

Kip ducked his head and didn't answer.

Jess asked: "Were you scared?"

"To death." His voice sounded hollow.

She turned to him, and just for a moment they were both thinking the same thing: how frightened they'd been and how it could've gone badly and how lucky they were, with the baby born and the mom okay, with food for everyone and a warm place to stay.

He looked like he had the same empty panic-place in his chest. Jess's tears choked out, stinging hot. Kip's thin face convulsed and they grabbed each other.

He never sobbed, or said anything, but she could feel

his ragged gasps. He held her for long minutes until she calmed down. Or maybe he was holding on to her.

"Caught up with me," she gasped. She dug some tissues out of her coat pocket. They sat shoulder to shoulder and stared out over the lobby.

"I kept asking why I got myself into that. I wanted Marcus Welby, M.D., to come in and take over. If that baby hadn't started breathing, I don't know what I would have done."

It hadn't gone wrong, but Jess wished for more reassurance. She was scared. She wanted something more, to cover up the fears and hold the joy. She wanted someone to put his arms around her and say it was all going to be okay. Because it was great! It was too exhilarating. She wanted to celebrate, to dance, to float like a soap bubble. She wanted to sing.

She turned to Kip, saw the shadow of his dark beard and the flush of his cheeks, the black hair fallen over his forehead, his gray eyes. Maybe he needed something more, too.

Then he turned and stroked her cheek and kissed her softly. He put his arm around her shoulders and squeezed her in a buddy hug. She put her arm around his back and shifted closer.

"I've got to be in Casper in two days. I'm going to be late for my first job." Once she said that she knew that it didn't make sense. She was crying and she wanted to laugh. "I hate to drive in the mountains and my feet are always cold and this is too much, too much." She giggled and sobbed. He held her and didn't once act impatient.

She wrapped her sleeping bag around them both. He kissed her again, and she said, "Are you glad to see me or is that your Boy Scout knife?"

He laughed.

She took his face in her hands, brushed his dark hair back from his forehead, and they kissed again. They tried to get comfortable against the wall.

"I want to kiss you," he said.

"We just did."

"I mean seriously."

She looked at him. She thought he was brave and helpful. Surely a man who delivered a stranger's baby was trustworthy. Clean. Honest. Reverent.

"Do nice girls?" he asked.

"Not here," Jess said.

"Do you want to?" He grinned, teasing.

"Doesn't make any difference if I did."

"If there was someplace?"

"You're making me uncomfortable."

He was silent. She hesitated, then said, "Probably." This was crazy. She was a sensible person, a recent college graduate, who never let herself get carried away. She didn't do these things.

This was something she could never explain to her mother: spending the night wrapped in a sleeping bag with a guy she had just met. It felt natural to be beside him, as though they had done it for years.

He squeezed her again and after a while they dozed off, wrapped up together in her sleeping bag. In the morning they exchanged phone numbers and left as soon as the highways were opened.

# 2

*Jessica Shelby had just* gotten back to her apartment in Casper after spending three months monitoring observation wells in the Powder River Basin for the U.S. Geological Survey. She loved driving the Survey pickup into the back country, bouncing over ranch roads and measuring water levels in the wells with another hydrologist.

Occasionally they sampled water from a rancher's well, pumping out three times the volume of the water in the well to get clean aquifer water for the sample. They filtered and acidified the water, then filled, capped, and labeled the sample bottles for common constituents or trace metals. Sometimes they were out so late the post office was closed and they had to go to the back door to mail boxes and coolers of samples to the Survey Lab in Denver. The data they collected was analyzed and written up in reports on water resources, which the Survey prepared.

Jess's title was hydrologist, and it had been a cold week on the Powder River west of Gillette. Her social life was a cowboy bar in Gillette, where she could get a good meal after cleaning up at the motel. Jess was glad there was one other trailblazing woman at this office. She and Evie Bylenowski could do fieldwork together, and the wives of the men in the office couldn't complain about her being out with their husbands. She went with men as often as with Evie, however. They would prove that women could do this work, as professionals and as equals. It felt like an uphill trek, but she was out in the field—in empty, beautiful, open country—doing work she loved.

She answered the knock at the door, and her heart jumped when she saw who was there.

"Hi." Kip stood on her doorstep with three camera bags and a backpack.

She gripped the doorknob to keep her balance. She stared. Then she gestured for him to come in.

She hadn't heard from him since they had parted in Socorro after the blizzard. Now it was March. She had been swept up by the demands of her new USGS job and hadn't been home more than a few consecutive days since she'd arrived. Had he phoned? She might not have been home. She had dialed his Washington, D.C. number twice but had never gotten an answer.

"Come in," she said.

"I just happened to be in the neighborhood." He grinned, but looked unsure.

"Two thousand miles from home?"

"Well, I've got this assignment. I'm going to be out here for a while."

"You never phoned."

He shrugged. "I phoned, but didn't get you. I was taking a chance you'd be glad to see me after three months."

"I *am* glad. But surprised."

Jess made coffee to cover her nervousness, the way a cat cleans herself, as he sat on her couch and told her he just got into town.

"How long will you be here? Where are you staying?"

"I don't know yet. Mostly, I wanted to see you first."

Jess felt her breath catch. The coffee mug shook a little in her hands. This was the way it was supposed to be in the movies, only there was no sound track, just Oscar Peterson on her old record player. And she didn't have any makeup on and she was wearing jeans and a sweatshirt.

"You never wrote," he said. "I wasn't sure."

"Neither did you."

"Yes, well." And he ducked his head. It was a boyish gesture, almost calculated.

"I phoned," she said.

"I was out on assignment a lot," he said.

"What are you going to do here?"

"I've got an assignment from Sarah Brocklein."

"For?"

"Wildlife photographs."

"For?"

"Children's books."

"And how long will you be here?"

"At least through November."

"Great," she murmured. "You'll love it out here. Wyoming is wonderful. Do you have a deadline?" She was having trouble concentrating on what he said. She felt her body soften. Her muscles relaxed, but her heart speeded up.

"The deadline is a year from now, but I need to be here through fall, about nine months, because I need different seasons to get different animals. I've got enough money, I think, for nine months. If I don't buy too much film."

"I was going to Thermopolis this weekend. Why don't you come with me? They've got mineral pools. It would be fun."

"That sounds great." Kip looked at her as though he were trying to memorize her face.

"Well, then it makes sense for you to stay here just for tonight. I don't have much room, but you're welcome. I have no idea how you find the animals there, though."

"Well, I know some wildlife people who know where the animals are, and I know the textbook habitat information and how they live. Mostly, it's finding a good place and sitting until you get a chance at a shot. And taking enough pictures."

"Isn't that hard?"

"No. Lots of people wonder how I can call it an occupation since most of the time I'm doing nothing."

"Why you? Most photographers fresh out of school don't get an assignment like this—carte blanche and all the money."

"Sarah was at school during Journalism Week, a big deal in the spring. She saw my horse picture."

"One picture?"

"Well, it won a prize. Four white horses. I got up before dawn every morning until the light was right, behind the trees, and the horses were running. On a farm outside of town. God, it was great! I felt like I was the only person awake in the world. When it got light enough I started shooting. And eventually, I got this great shot." He stopped, remembering. Then he went on. "Sarah is gambling I can do it. If I can't, she hasn't wasted much money. Much to me, but not to her."

"How do you sit still for a long time?"

"I meditate," he said with a grin.

They sat down on her couch, and he crossed his legs, joined thumb and forefinger in a yogic gesture, and rested his hands, palms up, on his knees.

Jess, flustered, stood up, turned away, turned back. If she looked at him he would know what she was thinking.

"I meditate on holy things," said Kip.

He reached for her and she moved closer. When he touched her she vanished, like ice on a grill. She stood beside him, looking down at him, waiting. He reached between her legs, rested his palm on her tailbone, then urged her toward him. He untangled his legs and she half-fell on top of him, laughing. She pinned his hands against the couch and kissed him fiercely.

Eventually he struggled free then pulled her back to him. They rolled one way, then the other, almost fell off the couch, and all of Jess's warm, damp places exploded, died and began again with Kip. They moved together like one body. No talk. She could only laugh or moan. Only afterward did they make their way to the bed.

In the middle of the night she awoke to find him sitting cross-legged, "meditating" again.

"Can't you sleep?" she mumbled.

"Don't want to."

She sat up, kissed him and fell back on her pillow utterly replete. Why was he complicated?

"What are you reading about?"

Jess looked up from the book. "Fetterman Massacre. It happened up in Story, not too far from the Buffalo office."

"You don't have to bone up to live in Wyoming."

"History is interesting."

"Get your stuff and we'll go to the pool," said Kip. He emptied his backpack on the hotel dresser top and put back inside it his trunks, a towel, and a bottle of shampoo.

"Let me finish this chapter." She ignored his aggrieved sigh as he sat down and stared out the window. His toe counted an impatient rhythm. Why did she feel guilty when she did what she wanted? He wanted her attention when he was around. She wanted to be with him, but she didn't want to abdicate herself entirely.

When she finished, she marked her place with a grocery receipt and rose to pack her things.

The Plaza Hotel, built around World War I, was a U-shaped, two-story stucco building on one edge of the state park in Thermopolis. They had a WC and a sink in their room, and the bathroom was down the hall.

None of the towels matched, and the bedspread was thin, but their meticulously clean room looked out on the park where fresh snow smoothed into melted drifts. The owner's kids played in the courtyard between the wings of the building, and soaks and massages were offered on the premises. In front of the hotel a bubbler fountain poured sulfurous water that tasted poisonous, not therapeutic.

"Star Plunge or the other one?" asked Kip.

"Star. I like the whirlpool. And it smells good."

"You smell good," he said and nuzzled under her right ear.

"That gives me goosebumps," she said, shivering.

Jess wrapped her arms around Kip, always surprised at his strength, and she pulled him against her so she could feel the play of muscles in his back.

"We could swim later," he offered.

Jess started unbuttoning his shirt.

Later they walked across the paths of Hot Springs State Park. She could see patches of grass in the snow. Jess thought they must water it all summer. No grass in Wyoming was that green otherwise. This park, with its old-fashioned hotel, state bathhouse, and commercial pools, had the look of an oasis. The Big Horn River curved around the park, and the hot mineral water ran out of the side of the hill.

The park was clean and well kept and a little artificial, as public parks always are—neat sidewalks, parking lots, bronze signs on the fountains and the bathhouse. The Tepee Fountain, a fifteen-foot-high phallic mineral deposit, dripped obscenely as they walked past.

"Have you been far away?" Kip's voice was gentle against the murmur of the water.

Jess opened her eyes and smiled. She sat on a ledge in the hottest part of the big pool, her back against a jet of hot water. Her long hair was wet and hung plastered halfway down her back.

He picked up one of her feet and massaged it under water. He knew the places that tickled, the places that were erogenous, and the places that were callused. He was absently rubbing the erogenous places. The steamy water and the echoing sounds in the huge cavernous room lulled her.

"I've never had my feet rubbed in a public place," she said. Kip grinned mischievously and tickled them, breaking the spell.

How long would this honeymoon feeling last? When she was alone with Kip, everything else fell away. No profession, no responsibilities, no ambitions, no plans — just the two of them skin to skin. Time stopped. She was complete. Was that love or the lovemaking? How could the whole of her life be reduced to the fifty-four by seventy inch bed, the lovers' field?

When they made love she was perfectly centered. When she orgasmed, synapses fired again and again, and all circuits blew. She imagined her central nervous system cleared of all tension, erased like chalk on a board. Muscles released. Blood flowed without hindrance. Bones rested untroubled. Her brain stilled. She was mute. Only skin sensations, smells, and murmurs penetrated her consciousness. She sank into a stupor of content.

She didn't need this distraction. She was beginning a demanding career and needed her energy for that. Besides, she was in the field for weeks at a time, and he would be gone, too. Don't get too involved, she warned herself. You know you tend to go overboard, then you're hurt and disappointed. Keep it light.

So they had driven to Thermopolis that morning and would stay overnight. In spite of being on the road so much for her job, she still wanted to explore Wyoming.

They didn't know how to act yet. She had to leave for Gillette on Monday, and he had appointments in Laramie. They anticipated a rendezvous next weekend. Could it work this way? He was impatient when she read, but she needed some down time, some room to breathe, after depleting her energy at work. She needed not to bend too readily to him. There was so much to learn, and everything was new.

They had driven down the Wind River Canyon looking

for hawks, and he had spent an hour nearly motionless, at the base of a cliff, watching them circle. She had stayed in the car, trying to read and wondering how he could be so restless at home and so focused when he worked. She didn't think she would get used to the camera perpetually around his neck or within reach.

This felt too good too soon and not solid enough. They had talked late the night before, trying to fill in all the blanks in each other's stories. She discovered why he wasn't drafted since he'd graduated last June. A heart murmur—not serious, but sufficient to keep him out of Vietnam.

He had learned that she had an M.A. from University of Texas-El Paso. But they really didn't know each other very well. They were terribly polite about the bathroom and making coffee for each other.

"I'm a prune," Jess said, holding her wrinkled hand palm up to prove it. "I'm going to get dressed."

"I'll meet you out front," Kip said. He looked like an Indian today, with a shock of straight black hair matted against his forehead. He looked like a hoodlum when he needed a shave. Sometimes he looked like a young Moses. He was Sean Raphael Kilpatrick and she wanted to know him better.

# 3

*Jess was hungry when* they got out of the pool, but Kip wanted to take pictures. He dressed in their room, picked up two cameras, and disappeared without a word, heading toward the steaming mineral terraces—rounded white deposits where water flowed down to the river.

After an hour Jess got hungry enough to walk into town to one of the cafes. She bought a copy of the *Thermopolis Independent Record* and ordered dinner. She was furious and disappointed, and the walk wasn't enough to calm her down.

This distracted artist routine was crap. Who did he think he was? Just go off and leave her like that. And after they'd had such a good time. Why had she trusted him? Just because she wanted to be with him she had persuaded herself he was acceptable. She'd gone from utterly relaxed to totally ticked off.

She went back to their room and picked up her book. He returned three hours later when he had run out of light.

He was wet and shivering, his lips blue, his teeth chattering, and his clothes soaked. But she wasn't going to let pity keep her from telling him off.

"Don't do that again."

He looked blank.

"Don't go off like that without explaining. It was inconsiderate. *You* are inconsiderate. I thought you cared more about me. Next time, I won't be here when you get back."

"Hey, wait a minute. You're mad?"

"Of course! Nobody treats me like this."

"Sorry, sorry, sorry," he said. He put his cameras on the dresser. "Did you bring any soft cloth, like an old shirt?" He stood dripping, shivering, and took the cameras out of the cases, before even taking off his coat. "I've got to get this lens dry. I don't know if the film's ruined. I dropped this camera and if water got inside, well I've got to dry it out." He ran a finger along the chrome-finished brass strip where the halves of the camera met.

"Here's some Kleenex," she said. "What happened to you?"

"I fell in." He grinned. One wet glove dripped from a parka pocket. He carefully, carefully wiped the lens, opened the camera to remove the canister of exposed film, and wiped carefully, carefully inside.

He shivered uncontrollably.

"Get out of those wet clothes," Jess said.

He put the camera down long enough to get undressed. It was the first time he'd undressed himself since he came. He stood at the dresser stark naked, his little white butt goosebumped, nuts shriveled, and wiped the camera again inside and out. Then he took the other, dry camera, unwrapped the chamois protecting it, took it out of its case and carefully, carefully dabbed its lens.

Jess didn't know whether to be angry or laugh. He looked like a blue heron, standing naked on one foot, skin white and wrinkled from the water. Eventually he decided the lenses were dry and ran hot water in the sink. "I need to go back in the pool to warm up."

Jess was not going to feel sorry for him.

"Take a hot shower." She was still angry, but concerned that he'd catch cold. He pulled the bedspread off to wrap himself for the trip down the hall.

When he was showered and warm and wrapped in the bedclothes, he told her what had happened. "I was climbing on the mineral terrace . . ."

"I thought there were signs saying Keep Off."

"No, they have places you can walk out on. I talked to the guy at the state building. It wasn't going to parboil me if I got onto the terraces. And it was slippery, and the hot water is running. I got some shots, then I slipped and went down and got wet. Thank God I didn't damage the cameras. When I'd shot up that roll, I wrapped up one camera, then I went down to the river. Water is the hardest thing to photograph. It absorbs light. It changes light. And this mineral water was stranger than anything."

Kip started shaking again.

"You need something hot to eat. Get dressed and we'll go into town."

"I don't have any dry pants."

"What? You didn't bring a change of clothes?"

"I brought clean underwear but no pants. I wear a pair of Levis a week, then I wash them."

"You want to wear mine?" Jess had brought a complete change of clothes, plus extra underwear.

"I guess." Kip looked doubtful. He pulled on the jeans, and they ballooned around his hips.

"I'll donate some of my fat next time I lend you my Levis," she said.

Kip looked embarrassed.

"Do you want me to go get you a sandwich and coffee so you don't have to go out?"

"No, no. Probably nobody'll notice."

"They see everything during hunting season."

Over steak in the restaurant Kip continued: "It wasn't bad where the water was warm, but it was cold down at the river. There was just a trace of steam rising from the hot water. I couldn't find a place to stand where I was in line with the light and I could see into the water.

"If you don't find that place, the water is opaque, it looks dead. I didn't have a polarizing filter with me. I couldn't get into position, the water was reflecting the light, and I fell again. Where the hot water goes into the cold river is beautiful. Probably nobody but me and the park superintendent has seen it since the Indians were here."

Jess didn't care about water, but she loved to watch Kip's face as he talked. It was full of life and enthusiasm, like a child's.

"Probably nobody wanted to," she said.

"The Indians'd soak in the hot water on the terraces, then go down to the river and cool off. Steam and minerals and the sound of the river—it was great!"

Jess sighed. She felt like Winnie the Pooh's nanny. Kip's hair dried with a cowlick standing up in back, and she could scarcely keep her hand from stroking it down. They were the only people left in the restaurant.

After they paid, they found a friendly looking bar with stuffed heads and photographs of people displaying trophy animals decorating the walls. The Beatles sang "Yesterday," and a gust of fresh air came in with each new customer.

"The light changes," Kip said. "I think it's the red sandstone or whatever it is in the hills. It's as though the whole world turns red."

Jess had noticed the beautiful sunset, but never noticed that the light changed color.

"I got the reddish light and the water foaming down the river and the hot water running in and the steam and the terraces. It was wonderful. When I ran out of light and film, I noticed I was cold."

"I'm glad you noticed. I can just see the headline: *PHOTOGRAPHER FREEZES ON MINERAL TERRACE*."

"Uh, you're still mad." He sipped his scotch.

"I thought we came here to have a good time together. I'm glad you're excited about your work, but you just went off. You didn't tell me how long you'd be or where you were going. I didn't know whether to worry that you'd drowned or be angry."

"I'm sorry. I didn't know until I got into it how long it would take."

"You lose track of time."

"I can't help it. If I don't concentrate, I can't do it at all."

"Next time, let me know what to expect. I won't worry about you. I won't feel ignored." She was still ticked, but he apologized and he had a good reason and really she should be gracious about it.

Kip, finally warm and fed, was unstoppable. "Water is the hardest thing to do, water and snow. They change. Water bends light." He put a red plastic swizzle stick into his drink and Jess saw the stem separate, a mystery from childhood. "But it's alive, too. Water pollen. It moves, it changes, it catches the light, sometimes it keeps it, sometimes it sends the light back. I have to find crosslight or it looks like nothing.

"My mother tells me she couldn't get me out of the bathtub when I was little. She gave me swimming lessons early because I wasn't afraid and thought I could breathe underwater. A couple of years ago when I was in school, it was Thanksgiving break and it was too far to go home from school, so I went to Boonville where there was a bridge over the Missouri River. I was absolutely sure the river was going to freeze that day. It had been truly cold for a week and I wanted to catch the ice floes as they formed."

Jess shook her head.

"I put on so many clothes I barely fit behind the steering wheel. I had cameras, film, handkerchiefs because my nose runs in the cold. I walked about two-thirds of the way across the bridge and it was slippery as hell. It was made of steel grid and water was supposed to run out between the spaces in the grid. I guess it did, but when it got cold, the metal froze the water fast, before the roads. I slipped and slid and finally got where I wanted to be and I stood there. And stood there. And I hunkered down, then I tried to sit, then I stood up again. Brass monkey time. I took a picture. I waited. No change. The water wasn't freezing. I took another picture. No ice. The clouds came in and the light changed and I tried to put a filter on and my hands were cold and stiff and I dropped the damned thing into the river! Expensive Leica filter. And the river never did freeze, of course."

"What kind of pictures did you get?"

"Nothing. River jes' keep rollin' along. I blew up one shot and put it over my desk. To remind me that I'm not as smart as I think I am."

"Wait till summer and you see the irrigation sprinklers," Jess said. He looked puzzled. "The ranchers irrigate hay for cattle. Long row of pipes with water, like fountains. They're beautiful. What would you do if you could get it all on film?"

"I don't know. A water portfolio. I can make pretty pictures, but I don't know if anybody would be interested."

"Check out the state tourism people—maybe they want some river pictures for brochures. Wouldn't hurt." She considered what he had said. "Was it worth it, freezing on the bridge today?"

"Sometimes it's not—the pictures come out shitty or they're just okay and I can't sell them. I seem to have to make all the mistakes before I figure out how to do it right. But I keep trying and keep trying because one time in five or one time in twenty, or a hundred, you get these sweet shots, everything just the way you want it, and it all works and they get published and you get paid for it. And your name sideways in six-point type next to the photograph. Like a salesman—you make enough calls, eventually you'll sell something."

Jess felt troubled but couldn't identify the feeling, that shiver of apprehension when something is going wrong and you don't know what it is so you can't stop it. Why couldn't she just enjoy the moment, get as absorbed as Kip did when he looked through the camera?

"I had another idea, Jess." He leaned forward with a conspiratorial grin. "Remember in Socorro, when we met in January, that woman having a baby?"

"How could I forget?" Jess saw the dim room, felt the anxiety, heard the baby's cry, and her heart lifted.

"Why not do it again?"

"You're nuts. No woman would agree to having a

baby on the floor of an abandoned hotel in a snowstorm."

"No, I mean in a hospital, all antiseptic, with doctors and everything. But this time there's light and I photograph the whole process. What do you think?"

"I think it's a great idea, but how do you find a woman willing to let you shoot up her legs? You'd have to get permission from the hospital. Find a willing obstetrician. Get the husband to agree. Taking the pictures would be the easy part."

"I hadn't thought of that. It'll take a while to set up. I need to find a pregnant woman. By the time she's ready, maybe I can get it all arranged."

"Will it be worth all the trouble?"

"You never know. It might be a bust and it might be wonderful. I could get it all arranged, then nobody'd publish them. I don't even know if the editor in Casper would run them if I did do it. I have to take a lot of pictures, try a lot of experiments—you don't just take one picture and get it right the first time."

They had a couple of scotches in the bar, a dim, smoky room full of other tourists and people from town who knew each other. The lights behind the bar lit their faces and Jess could see more stuffed heads, traps, and snowshoes decorating the walls. "King of the Road" and country hits competed with The Byrds and Rolling Stones. Then Kip put his hand on her arm and squeezed, so they left and walked through the cold, nighttime streets to their room.

"You can't be a hydrologist. Girls aren't scientists," Kip steered Jess's battered Chevy across the rangeland east of Shoshoni, the ruddy sunset over his shoulder turning the grass claret. When he glanced across at her he saw that her brown hair looked red in the light and her eyes looked deep.

"It doesn't take a lot of muscle to measure wells," she said. "I can lift a hundred-pound cement sack, when we put in wells. I've got to, to prove a woman can do the job. And I can."

"How did you end up a scientist? I mean you're entitled to do whatever you want." Kip frowned. That didn't come out right. The hills' shadows changed as the light slid out of sight behind them.

"I took a geology survey class and got interested. Then Dr. Hedges sort of took me under his wing."

"That must have been a help. Cliff Edom sort of takes all the photography majors under his wing."

"I love it, plus Mrs. Hedges made it possible."

"How?"

"She is *Mrs.* Doctor Hedges—has the same Ph.D. in the same subject as *Mr.* Doctor Hedges. She helps him prepare his articles, writes them sometimes. He's the department chair, so she does social things. She doesn't get her name on anything. Plus, when he goes in the field, she goes with him because she knows what he's doing. Having her along meant I could go without a lot of gossip—senior professor, bunch of randy college boys, and one girl.

"How did she help?" Kip asked.

"A million ways." Jess thought about it. "She told me what to expect—male attitudes. How to do things. A friend of mine in vet school had to sew up the pockets in her coveralls so her petticoat wouldn't show through the slot they leave so men can get into their inside pants pockets.

"Mrs. Hedges—Ericka—taught me how to go to the

bathroom in the field with a bunch of men around. Practical things like that. She taught me how to stand up for my ideas. Men don't hear you, when you're a woman. You can say something and nobody notices, and ten minutes later a man will say the same thing and everybody thinks he's a genius. How do you get credit? How do you get men to take you seriously?"

"How?"

"Do the job professionally. Be competent. Don't preach."

"Do I listen?"

"You better." Jess meant it but tried to keep her voice light. "I suggested this safety thing—put the generator in a tray or on a pallet. Nobody would do it, then one of the new guys dropped it, hurt himself, and everybody decided it was a good idea. When I was afraid and wanted to do it, it wasn't important."

Jess took a deep breath, trying to let go of the memory. This week's *Life* magazine carried an ad of a woman in high heels and impeccable dress and bouffant hair staring at a flat tire that she was clearly too perfectly groomed to change by herself. Most men called women "girls" and treated them like retards. She still saw articles in the papers and magazines and on TV of The First Woman Who— or The First Black Who— .

"I get tired of fighting," Jess said. "But I have to do the job and stand up for myself."

"Girls aren't supposed to be pushy," Kip said.

"If a man acted that way you would say he's aggressive. It's just that you're not used to it. Yet." Jess smiled. "I shouldn't let you call me *girl*."

"Not even, 'Girl, I can't wait to make love with you'?"

"I guess that's okay," she said. She reached over and ran her hand down his thigh.

"Women aren't supposed to make as much money for the same work, either," she went on. "And that's bullshit." Jess remembered that dragged-out feeling when she had had to stand up for herself, talk calmly when she wanted to cry, be logical when the men were acting irrationally. Would Kip turn out like that? she wondered.

"Once the men decide I'm no big threat, they sort of loosen up and we get the work done. Then it's all worth it. I love getting all the information together, analyzing it, working it all out. I'm out somewhere so beautiful I can't believe they're paying me to be there. It's a great feeling when you complete a project. It's something that helps people, in the long run. I love it. Not the way you love making pictures, but this is what I want to do. I wanted it enough to go to grad school, to put up with the masculine shit, make my way."

They were silent for a while. The landscape stretched time as they drove between cities, and the twenty- and forty-mile vistas opened Jess's heart. She wouldn't go back to Kansas City and the low-hanging sky. Today, the distance gave them time to talk in the car. "It's hard for me to explain the freedom."

"In a federal bureaucracy?"

"I'm on my own. I'm out in the middle of nowhere, without another soul. I can do whatever I want. And I like what I do. Miles from the highway on some watershed, with an elk about half a mile away and a 360-degree sunset."

"I can understand that part," Kip said. "I can sort of understand why you have to prove yourself. I remember going down to Mississippi and all these Eastern college kids were doing voter registration."

"You could have gotten killed!"

"Not me. I'm an observer. Always fade into the background. Anyway, I noticed they talked about equality for blacks, but the girls still cooked and ran the mimeograph machines. They 'balled' a lot, but it was up to the girl to have a diaphragm or buy rubbers."

"At least you buy your own."

"I'm getting fast."

"Almost as fast as you load your camera."

He looked at her and they laughed.

*Kip had that sinking feeling* that he couldn't produce the goods. He had talked his way into this contract, convinced Sarah that he could do the job and he didn't know how. *Face it, kid, you're afraid you can't deliver. They'll find you out. You'll be blackballed in New York and never work and end up taking school photos for yearbooks.*

He sat in his dusty green Merc and looked at the list of appointments. Too many U. of Wyoming professors. He would never absorb enough information fast enough. He would run out of money before he finished. There were too many animals. Wyoming was too big.

He should be in New York, he thought. Nobody got famous out here. He hoped that people here were friendly. If you could find somebody who lived in the area, they could usually tell you more than professors.

Jess was unusual to like the outdoors. He wondered what all the dust in the air in Laramie did to the sky.

He'd have to take some shots this afternoon, as the sun went down. Filters? How could he brace the camera in wind like this?

He spread his notes out on the seat beside him. He labeled them and filed them in folders. Then he went to the college bookstore for reference books and more folders. When he got back to the car, he still had twenty minutes before he talked to the professor who he hoped would tell him where to find peregrine falcons.

Kip looked at the backseat. He always operated on the assumption that anyone might break into his car to steal his expensive cameras. In D.C., this was a reasonable assumption. So he accumulated trash to camouflage the camera cases and make his car unattractive. He carried much insurance.

He had lived happily this way until the weekend before, when Jess had said she'd rather drive her Chevy to Thermopolis. When he had defended his technique, she had pointed out that he could lock his cameras in the trunk, out of sight. She hadn't criticized him, but he felt reprimanded.

The fragile rationalization collapsed. He was meticulous, even fastidious, about his work. The cameras were checked after each trip, the prints developed with finical care, the negatives filed in sleeves. He supposed he could clean the car.

He began by shaking out a grocery bag and stuffing into it: last Sunday's *Casper Tribune* and *Billings Gazette*, including all advertising supplements; empty Cheez-It boxes, and one that had held animal crackers, paper sacks and used tissues. He shook the Ritz box and ate the last handful of fragments. The sack was filling up, so he stomped the boxes flat and picked up cartons and empty beer and soft drink cans and bottles off the floor. He studied a scarf left by an old girlfriend, sniffed it, then pushed it into the now full sack.

He looked for another sack but found none, so he walked to the nearest trash can, dumped the debris out and went back. This time he came up with old copies of *Time* and *Life* and *The New York Times Magazine*. He decided to keep a couple of photography magazines. He dusted a metal box of 4" x 6" cards, which contained his sales records and an address file. He threw out a dozen cheerful yellow and black film boxes, ripped wrappers, and black film cans without caps. He kept batteries and wires for shutter and flash. One sound tripod and one crippled one.

All this he stashed in an empty camera case, then rearranged his suitcases and boxes of books to make room in the trunk. He locked that case and another, containing a Nikon, in the trunk. He would have to quit putting film in the trunk in the summertime, but it would be okay for a while.

When he finally finished cleaning the car interior was still dusty, but neater. He washed his hands on his way to the appointment.

It was early March, and the sun shone as the wind lashed through the campus. Kip expected it to get warmer, but the professor had said it snowed in May for sure and sometimes in June, especially at high altitudes. He would need long johns, a sheepskin jacket, a camp stove, and a better hat. He discovered an outdoors store, but the prices took his breath away. Maybe the prices were hiked there since it was a college town. He'd wait and see if he could save any money by buying in Casper.

Kip considered camping but decided he could afford a motel room that night. Snow was predicted, and he was afraid of the wind. Jess was gone until Thursday night. At this time tomorrow he would have enough information to plan the next six months. First a time schedule for habitat, migrating, birth, and rutting. Then he'd match the dates with places, plug in the contacts, and draft letters. He needed a secretary. After tomorrow's appointments, he'd drive back to Casper, get out Jess's typewriter, and go to work.

Maybe he *could* fill this contract.

If he didn't freeze. If the animals would cooperate.

Even iffier was Jess. He was staying with her temporarily. She seemed pleased that he was here. She said she was in love with him, which scared him, but what else do you call it? He was in love with her, he guessed. Neither of them seemed able to ask what it meant. Or how long it would last.

He wanted to move in so he could spend more time with her, but that was her choice. People he knew at home got married. People in New York did whatever they wanted to, he heard. Here in Wyoming he wanted to live with Jess and make love every chance they got. He hoped his conscience wouldn't prick him. Would hers bother her? He knew people at college who had done it. When he had graduated from MU in '64 there was a street of apartments known as Sin City where unmarried couples lived. Hippies and bikers did it all the time. It was time that nice middle-class boys from Chevy Chase did it.

He didn't know if Jess had misgivings about what they were doing. She said she loved him, then she put a disclaimer on it: "That doesn't mean I expect anything." But she had to expect something. If not a long-term arrangement, then disappointment. Heartbreak. Tragedy. No, tragedy was for Shakespeare, not real people.

What did he expect from her? Good sex. Demands? Tears? Always tears. The girl either said good-bye or started hinting about a ring and he said good-bye. He had met a girl at college just before they graduated. Would she have broken her engagement for him? He had never asked.

Kip had gone to school with girls who were there to find husbands. Jess wasn't looking for one. In fact, a husband would get in her way. Kip would get in her way.

He wasn't sure he liked that part. He wanted someone dependent on him . . . for what? He'd run the other way if Jess turned clingy. He wasn't ready to support a wife. He could barely support his cameras and their insatiable demands for film. Someday, when he was older, he wanted a woman who would stay home and have kids. And do the cooking and housekeeping and all that stuff.

He did love Jess. There was something absolutely authentic about her that drew him to her like a magnet. He had no doubt that she was human and capable of lying and cheating and playing dirty. And she would, if pushed. But she would suffer over it. When it came to the two of them and what they had together, she was absolutely sincere. He called her Straight Arrow, faithful companion to the daring and resourceful camera rider of the plains.

"Yes, Kemo Sabe," said Jess. "You can sleep on snow. You need insulation, and a way to stay out of the wind. I'll lend you my tent, but it's not very good for winter."

"Do you know how expensive they are? It's awful." He looked up from a Sears catalog.

"Go to the army surplus," she said. "Think of it as an investment—like buying a vacation house."

"Why don't people paint their tents?"

"Don't know."

"I mean the Indians painted tepees—all kinds of magic designs."

"Only anthropologists and archeologists like Indians. All the locals look on them as second class, the niggers of the west. They don't have any blacks to oppress, so they find somebody else to hate."

"You sound bitter."

"Just look at the history."

"Tell me." Kip put the book aside.

"Too long."

"How come you know all this stuff? I barely had time to read for classes."

"You go to school out west, you sort of have to learn it in self-defense. The natives think you're an ignorant Easterner. Besides, it's better than novels."

"I took esthetics. God, the reading. I was the only person in the history of journalism school to take it. But Cliff said to try it, so I did. I was the only undergraduate in the class with all these fine-arts types talking academic, the language of obfuscation."

"You just blew it," said Jess.

"What'd I do?" Kip asked. She was always catching him in some inconsistency.

"Most of the time you go around all innocent, pretending you're naive and don't know anything. It's a big scam to disarm people so you can take pictures. You charm the socks off them and they tell you their life stories. Then you slip up and use words like 'obfuscation' and I know you actually went to college. And took a class in esthetics."

He grinned. "Aced it, too."

She got down on the floor with him and thumbed through the catalog. "Did it help?"

"What?"

"The class."

"Actually, yes. It gave me some ideas, but nothing that shows up in the pictures. I want the camera to do more than catch the surface."

"Like Curtis."

Kip was surprised she knew Curtis's work—sepia prints of Indians taken early in the century.

"You do good portraits," Jess said.

"Thanks. I try to see inside."

"Lone Stranger steal souls."

"It doesn't work that way. You can have theory and you can have a good eye and you can study design and look at a million photographs, and there's still that moment. Either it comes or it doesn't. You catch it or you don't.

"Just think," he continued. "You're standing there with your camera up to your face. You've got the subject framed, he's standing still. How do you choose the one-millionth of a second that will be the right one? There's something Zen about it. No matter how hardheaded you are, you have to acknowledge the pure damned randomness of it.

"I look at you, and I want your beauty. I study you. I think about the light, the film, the exposure. I live with you and watch you, trying to figure out which expression, which gesture tells most about you."

"That makes me creepy-crawlie."

"It does? How?"

"It feels like voyeurism."

"It *is*. Esthetic voyeurism. Maybe I do steal souls."

"Are you really thinking about it all the time?" Jess asked.

"Just about."

"That's spooky." She sat up. "Makes me want to turn all the lights off so you'll stop."

"I'm in favor of that," he said as he slid his arm around her waist.

"When you get your camping gear together, we'll go up Casper Mountain and test it overnight. If we get too cold, we can just come home."

They stayed in each other's arms there on the floor on the Sears catalogue and ruined pages and pages of "Supplies, Camping."

"I've got a surprise," Kip said.

"What is it?" Jess checked her bag for extra socks and added a roll of toilet paper.

"Won't be a surprise if I tell you." Kip turned his back and continued to pack a cardboard box.

"Cardboard isn't very substantial."

"It'll do for tonight."

They drove up through the outlying suburbs in the foothills, then up Casper Mountain. The road hadn't been cleared, and the fresh snow slowed them. Jess was ready to stop at the first campground. They hadn't seen a soul.

"Not yet. I want to go higher," said Kip. "I found out where to go from the guys in the store, and it's farther up."

He turned off at an unmarked road and drove through some pines to a clearing where there was an abandoned cabin. The snow lay glistening and silent, unmarked except for tiny etchings by squirrels and birds.

He took his box out of the back and said, "We're going to the observatory."

"I didn't know there was an observatory up here."

They tramped through the snow around a picnic table, then walked out into the open. They could see the other side of the mountain fall away into the distance. Jess shivered. The air pierced like an ice shard, and stars glittered in the black sky. She watched as Kip spread a tarp, unrolled ground pads, then another tarp.

"I don't want to sleep here."

"This isn't for sleeping," he said.

When all was smooth, with the box weighing down one corner, he gestured for her to get on. She felt the thin ice crust over the snow break each place she stepped. Then Kip got on and pulled her down. They were on a raft floating in a sea of snow. He rummaged in his box and found a flashlight with red cellophane over the bulb end and a folded piece of paper.

"Any place you observe stars is an observatory," he said.

"Where's the star machine and the lecture?" Jess asked.

"You look at the real stars. I do the lecture. Here's a star map. First you find the North Star, then you follow a line down to here, and that's a constellation."

He turned on the red flashlight and showed Jess how to find the constellations. He knew all their names. After a while he showed her planets through a telescope. They were harder to find. The telescope was not a kid's toy, but a serious instrument in a heavy cradle.

"If it wasn't clear, with the moon down," said Kip, "we couldn't do this. Here, stop that when I'm lecturing."

"Sorry. I'll be good."

"Pay attention. Saturn should be just about here," he

said in his professor's voice, jabbing at the star map. He looked through the telescope, then showed her how to find the planet.

"Oh wow! It really has rings!"

"I put them on just for you."

"They're beautiful." She could scarcely breathe. "They shine. Like a diamond collar. Oh Kip!" Words failed. She squeezed him through his thick parka.

He got up and put away the star map and telescope and pulled a bottle from inside his parka. "Didn't want it to freeze," he said. Sitting crosslegged,he unscrewed the lid with clumsy hands, bit off one glove, and fished out the plastic loop. He took a deep breath, and blew a stream of bubbles.

Jess laughed with delight. She hadn't blown bubbles in years, and never at night. She loved to see them dancing away. Each sphere picked up stars and floated away tiny bits of light. The wind stole them, then one big bubble rolled over and over, drifting between the bright snow and the shimmering high-altitude stars.

She saw a meteor fall.

After a while Kip put the bottle in the cardboard box. As they lay in each other's arms Jess thought she would drown upward and swim into the stars flung above their observatory raft.

When they started shivering, they lit the Coleman lantern, pitched Kip's new tent, and got inside.

"It's too cold to get naked," she said. Her teeth chattered.

"Where there's a will, there's a way," he muttered as he twisted open the button on the waistband of her Levis, and tugged the zipper down. They fell around her knees, and he drew her panties down. Cold air hit warm skin. He got his jeans down, and his cold hands grabbed her and pulled her to him.

"Don't you want to?" he asked.

"Yes. You are—I mean, thank you. . . ." and she couldn't talk.

He kissed her, and she relaxed a little and they knelt on the sleeping bag and pretty soon things got warm and sweaty and he was right—there *was* a way.

She saw: his bony face, grinning. The dark hair falling in his eyes. She touched: navel dimple, skinny ribs, little ass. She breathed: coffee, lust, soap, cold. His breath was in time with hers, warm and damp, and then she was gone, falling off the mountain. And never hit bottom.

Later they zipped themselves into the double sleeping bag.

He grunted and pulled her into a spoon.

"Blew it again, I suppose," he said.

"You're not supposed to be an astronomy buff, too." She shifted around in the sleeping bag. "There's really no reason for you to find an apartment."

"Which means?"

"You're gone so much you'd hardly be living there."

"What're you trying to say?"

"You're not making it easy! Why don't you just leave your stuff in my apartment? Most of it's there anyway."

"Thanks, I thought you'd never ask," he said and squeezed her. "No. Really, I'm pleased. I want to stay with you but only as long as you want me to. Say the word and I'll leave."

Jess twisted around and kissed him, and he squeezed again.

She lay awake waiting for her feet to warm up. Kip could be endearing—as in this excursion. He had gone to some trouble to get everything together. Even soap bubbles! But Winnie the Pooh had forgotten glove liners and extra socks and ground pads.

She didn't understand him. How could he take hours developing prints and know that one negative would print up better than another? It was a wonder that he didn't have a camera on the snow raft.

She was conscientious, methodical, and organized, but not creative, except when it came to writing proposals for her office. She accepted the photographs she saw in magazines and didn't imagine that they could be any different until Kip showed her how.

Mug shots of people printed in the Casper paper looked like they should have numbers across their chests. Kip showed her some old shots he'd made of people whose house had burned—spot news. They were the same idea—people's faces, shot head-on with hardly any artificial lighting. But Kip's people looked, well, more *interesting*. He found shadows. He caught an expression that was guarded but not faked.

She wondered if his basic decency had something to do with the results. He respected his subjects. He saw the pain behind the tight lips and staring eyes. There was some of that in his animal pictures, as though he granted them dignity by not sentimentalizing them.

When he showed her his photographs, she saw, then, what he saw but still didn't understand how he got there, why he didn't think in the same visual cliches as most of the other people in the world.

Here in this tent, bagged together with him, she felt warm, secure, and loved. And still she knew something she tried to ignore: he would leave. If he were persistent —and he seemed to be—and lucky, his work could be published in national magazines. He was that good, and even she could see it.

# 5

*The Monday after* the Saturday night on Casper Mountain Jess left for Gillette. Kip took a portfolio down to the editor of the *Casper Star-Tribune* that afternoon and the editor agreed to look at any free-lance work he brought in. Kip never knew when spot news might come along while he was looking for wildlife. The editor gave tentative approval to the childbirth photo essay.

Neither Kip nor Jess would have chosen this on-and-off schedule, but this way they could assimilate what they learned between meetings.

Kip met disaster on his first solo trip.

"You look like you just lost your best friend," Jess said when he walked in.

"I ruined the Nikon." They ate dinner in silence.

"Do you need to replace it?" Jess hung up the dish towel and poured herself more coffee, then put the percolator back on the stove.

"The oil froze, and it jammed. It's too expensive to repair. I'd have to send it off." He clamped his teeth together.

"The camera freezes, your hands get cold. . . ."

"And the film breaks. And when I tried to blow snow off the lens, my breath condensed on it."

"That should get you some interesting effects," Jess said.

"It's not funny!"

"Sorry."

Jess thought for a couple of minutes. "Can you clean the oil out of the cameras? So there's none there to freeze?"

"I guess so," said Kip. He considered it. "Not good for the camera, but freezing isn't good, either."

"You need some way to keep everything warm," she said. "Put a heater in the camera case?"

"They have these hand heaters that use lighter fluid."

"Might work."

"The fluid seeps out of the cotton inside. It would get all over the stuff in the case."

"Let me think about it. Anybody can take pictures when the weather is nice and the sun shines."

The next night, after dinner, Jess said, "Don't do that." It was a blustery Sunday at the end of March, and they were both home. They stayed inside, away from the seventy-five mile an hour wind, grateful for the murmur of the furnace.

"Do what?" Kip mumbled. He wasn't really paying attention but was methodically checking cameras.

"Don't take pictures of me when I'm not ready."

"I'm not." He flipped open the back to show her it was empty.

"Sorry."

"What's wrong with my taking a candid shot now and then anyway?"

"I don't know. I just don't like it."

Jess turned the book face down beside her on the couch. She smoothed the India cotton spread she'd thrown over the sofa. She had bought a few things to brighten the furnished apartment—blue curtains in the kitchen and a throw rug for the bare bedroom floor. She admired people who could decorate, but it always seemed frivolous. And she had little talent for it. Maybe when she had more money, she'd get an unfurnished place and buy her own furniture.

"My grandma wouldn't let my grandfather take photographs of her, ever." Kip worked with a clean dish towel spread on the kitchen table. He picked up a toothpick and made a delicate swab with cotton. "As a result, there are only two or three pictures of her, and she lived with a photographer for forty-seven years."

"I didn't know your grandfather was a photographer."

"He took high school class pictures and wedding pictures and more pictures of me when I was little than you can imagine. Beautiful, studio quality pictures. I look like an angel. I always knew who I was because of those pictures, like mirrors."

"I bet."

"Now that I think of it, I knew it meant something out of the ordinary that my grandfather took my picture. Most of my friends had one or two good photographs in frames, then snapshots and school pictures. I had dozens, in a scrapbook with wooden covers and leather hinges and that funny porous paper and little corners holding the photographs in place."

"If he was so good why didn't your grandmother let him take more of her?"

"I always wondered—he probably used to take pictures when she didn't know it, or when she didn't want him to. So she just made him stop altogether."

"I like those shots you got when we were at Thermopolis. I look as beautiful as a movie star."

"I didn't print the ones where you didn't."

"Oh. I thought you made me look good because you love me."

"There's that."

Jess watched him clean each camera with care.

"If I tell you I'm taking your photograph, you stiffen up," he said.

"What?"

"You said, don't take your picture without permission."

"I just don't want you to catch me eating or getting out of the bathtub or doing something groty."

"Those sound interesting, actually."

"Kip!"

"If I promise I won't print any that are 'groty' will you agree?"

"No. It's like peeping. I'd never feel at ease if I knew you were clicking away. Promise you won't shoot me when I don't know it. I'll get used to you in time."

"Okay. I don't want you paranoid every time I pick up a camera."

"I'd never have any privacy. I'd feel like I had to wear makeup all the time around the house."

"That's the part I like—your face, as it is. In early morning light."

"That's terribly flattering."

"What do you mean?" Kip wished the question hadn't come up.

"Just let me know when you want to take pictures and I'll try to ignore you. If the pictures come out nice, I'll probably relax." She watched him wipe off the advance arm. "How long are you going to be in Yellowstone?"

"Couple of weeks. I can get winter photos and go back in the spring and summer for more. That's part of the deal—the publisher wants all seasons."

"How do you keep from scaring away the wildlife with the noise of the camera?" Jess asked.

"I can muffle it some. Sometimes it doesn't bother them, but with birds, it's one shot, crank, and they're gone. I'm going to switch to a single lens Minolta—practically no noise at all."

"So you'll be here till it snows again."

Jess felt sad. She didn't think she wanted to marry Kip, but she didn't want him to just leave, either. She was used to having him here, to talk to. She had lived alone all through graduate school, without even a roommate. And now she had somebody to look forward to coming home to.

She cooked for him when he was there. She remembered interesting things in her books about the West to mention to him. Like Cissy Patterson, the heiress, like Doc Holliday and Wyatt Earp. Stories about mountain men who came out for furs, by Vardis Fisher and A. B. Guthrie. Histories of Lewis and Clark and the Oregon Trail.

She didn't want to get clingy or demanding. They had agreed at the beginning they wouldn't entangle their lives. They'd be separate. When it worked to be together, they would, and when it didn't, they wouldn't. She didn't want to keep him there if he didn't want to stay.

She'd gotten a prescription for the Pill and never missed taking one. She kept the dispenser next to her toothbrush. That would be a cheap way to keep him. She wished she were incredibly lovable, then felt like a fool for being so unrealistic. He loved her the way she was and that was enough.

She knew she was supposed to make him marry her, or she was a slut and he was taking advantage of her and all the other phrases she had heard all her life. *Knock her up. Living in sin.* None of it seemed to apply to the things she was feeling.

She had gone through college and learned what was prescribed. She was sensible, down-to-earth, rational. She did cerebral work well and had an IQ of more than two standard deviations above the mean. But she couldn't classify emotions or graph them. They defied analysis.

She wanted a family and babies, someday, but she couldn't imagine not working. She loved her work. Maybe she was too selfish to get married. Maybe they were both too selfish. Or too self-absorbed. Or maybe she just lusted after Kip's body. Kip could go, and another man would come, and eventually she'd settle down.

But if this was just a fling, why the cold feeling in the pit of her stomach, the emptiness she was trying to cover? She could tell herself that she didn't want to get married yet and that she didn't know Kip well enough anyway, but her gut betrayed her with spasms of fear when she thought of him going back East.

She and Kip had seen friends slip into secure, boring job-and-marriage slots after college, and they both had resisted. They thought: We're exceptional. We don't have to follow the rules.

He kept his hair short. She wore a bra. But they were rebels. Out there in Wyoming she didn't have to face her mother's concerns about what the neighbors would think. She liked this arrangement, but *should* she like it?

"That's enough." Kip put each camera away, coiled the shutter release wire, snapped the exposure meter into its case, packed fresh film in the camera bags, and zipped them shut. He cleaned off the kitchen table and got a silver can from the fridge.

"Get me one, too," Jess said.

"Let's neck," he said, when he sat beside her on the sofa.

"Don't we have to go to the park and steam up the car windows?"

"I don't think so. We can pretend this is the front seat." He turned off the lamp on the end table. "There. It's dark."

"And warm." Jess snuggled next to him. She felt his heat through her crewneck sweater. She habitually wore one more layer than he did, just to stay even. And her feet were cold from October to May. She sat there thinking about metabolism and heat, then she sat up. "Body heat!" She turned to him. "That movie we saw. Cary Grant wanted body heat."

"Now what?"

"Keep the cameras next to your body."

"I don't think there's room inside my new sheepskin jacket."

"I'll need a new jacket next winter," Jess said. "I'll buy that one from you. You buy a new one, a fat man extra large." She felt excited. "And wear mittens."

"I can't work with mittens." Kip didn't share Jess's delight in solving problems like this.

"Wear glove liners underneath. When you get a camera out, take off the mittens, your hands will be warm."

"I'll drop the mittens, too."

"I'll put them on a string through your sleeves, like your mommy used to do."

"Can I afford this?"

"Sure. And replace the Nikon. I'll give it to you for your birthday."

"That's not till August."

"You need it now."

"I don't feel right about this."

"It's just your male pride."

"Maybe it's stupid, but I pay my own way."

"Don't be like this!"

"Like what?" He'd turned the lamp back on.

"Like a stupid macho idiot."

"Thanks a lot." Kip stood and walked into the kitchen. Jess followed him.

"I'm not being diplomatic or careful of your ego. I'm sorry, I tend to be bossy. But let me do this, please," she said.

"Say I do. Then I'd be in your debt."

"So what's a loan between friends? I want to help you."

"You want to own me." He glowered, stormy-eyed and sulky.

"Then don't. Ruin your chances for the photographs you want. Be proud. Be stupid!" Jess stomped back into the living room.

Kip pulled his coat and a muffler off a hook and the backdoor slammed behind him.

When he came back half an hour later his backpack and camera bags were stacked by the front door, along with a laundry basket filled with his clothes and odds and ends.

"You want me to leave?" he asked. He was calm and sounded surprised.

Jess had calmed down.

"Because I won't take a loan?"

"Because you won't talk it out. As much as I love

you, if we can't work out problems, I don't want it."

"I was afraid I'd lose my temper."

"Lose it."

"I'm afraid you'd—"

"What?"

"I don't know. I'm not very good, I mean, I don't like to show—"

"I'm not very good, either."

"I never had a girl before who said this. I just did my thing. When one of us got fed up, it was over. It's uncomfortable."

"Yes, but it's better if we talk before we get fed up. I don't know how. We'll have to make it up as we go along."

"Let's—"

They sat for a while, each staring into the distance. At last Jess stood, picked up the laundry basket, and took it back into the bedroom. When she came back they sat down at the kitchen table and decided she'd pay for what he needed now, and he'd pay her back when he got the money. If either one was unhappy, he had to tell the other how he felt, and the other had to listen.

"I want you to succeed," she said. "More than anything. I think you're good. It is my pleasure to do this."

"I realize you're being a friend, but it feels like you're running me. And I feel guilty. When I'm working, I never think of you. All I think about is what I'm doing.

"That doesn't do anything for my ego, but I don't care, as long as you think about me when we're together." Kip filled her mind during blank hours—long drives over the back roads, through the hills, across the grasslands.

"Uh, thanks, I guess." He thought for a moment, scowling. "I know this idea is good, but it doesn't feel right."

"It's new, it'll take a while. Let's do it anyway." She reached across the table and stroked his hand.

"How do we act after I tell you how I feel and you listen and so on?" he asked.

"I don't know. I'm still upset." Jess stood up and fussed at the kitchen sink.

"Take up where we left off?" Kip took her by the hand, and they sat down on the couch again.

"You bounce back fast."

"A photographer's attention span is only a one-twenty-fifth of a second."

"So where were we?"

"We were necking." Kip took a pull on his now-warm beer.

"You turned the light out. Are you going to put your arm across the seat top?"

"Sure. And casually let it fall on your shoulders."

"Do I scoot over near you or will you scoot out from under the steering wheel?"

"I'll scoot." He put his beer on the table. "I'll casually brush your breast as I reach for something in the glove compartment."

"I'll lean forward to change the station on the radio, and rest my hand on your leg."

"Then we'll kiss?"

"French kiss," said Jess. "That's what we called it in high school."

"Will you pull away if I try to pet?"

They began slowly, like teenagers experimenting, but necking was too slow. They'd already experienced much more. In a few moments Jess pushed Kip down and lay on top of him, toe to toe, belly to belly, kissing him. Her long hair brushed his face, and she laughed between kisses.

"I want to take a long time, make it last, but I can't wait," she said. "Can't wait."

"I'm not going to make any money," Kip said.

"On what?"

They were lying on her bed with sections of Sunday papers littering the floor around it. Summer leaves of box elder brushed the window. Cumulus clouds floated through the blinding sunlight. They had lived together four months.

Casper was a busy little town, and a center for oil drilling and cattle ranching, with not much to do on the weekends except go dancing at the Beacon Club. Sometimes they stayed in from Friday night till Sunday, when they finally wandered out for groceries and found a laundromat.

"The money from Sarah Brocklein isn't covering expenses. I bought the tent and stuff, and I had to buy a new Hasselblad. I'm squeaking through this winter, but next snow season is going to be expensive. Right now I'm spending it all on film."

Kip hated to admit it, but Jess was supporting him between checks, and it would go on for another six months. Without her, he wouldn't be able to do these photographs for Brocklein. He felt diminished, as though he should be killing the woolly mammoth and dragging it home to the cave. He should not let her pay the bills.

"Use less film," Jess suggested.

"Not acceptable. Sometimes I shoot a brick and only print a couple of shots."

"Twenty rolls? My, we're fussy."

"For Sarah, each shot has to be perfect—animal

shown in focus, habitat visible. Context. Not easy."

Sarah Brocklein had sent him brittle orange Thermofax copies of the two manuscripts so he would know what she wanted him to illustrate. The pages were dirty and the corners flaking from rereading. His first batch of prints got a "That's nice" response from Sarah. He didn't know if that was typical or just lukewarm, if he should be worried or not. He did try harder.

"You don't think of it as wasting film?"

Kip bristled. "That's how I work. I know how many mistakes I make before I get it right. All professional photographers use a lot of film."

"All right, all right. I was teasing."

"Well, to tell you the truth, I'm afraid I didn't get what I thought I had, or the timing was off, or the light just wasn't ever right. Sometimes I really don't know what I have until I print it." He thought for a moment. "I notice you use a lot of paper."

"Me?"

"Typing up reports."

"Oh, well. That's different. I don't know what I think until I see what I say." She pursed her lips to keep a straight face. "I know you have to get it right. I have to get it right, too. Draft after draft, if that's what it takes. It takes paper and time, always more time than I think it'll take. Those reports are our 'product'—they have to be good. And peer review will kill you if you don't get it right."

"Always," he agreed.

"I'm often afraid I'll run out of brain power before I get all the ideas down," she said. "Or that I left out something crucial. Or misinterpreted what I saw." She rested her hand on his chest. "I understand not feeling sure of yourself."

"I've *got* to do a good job for Sarah because she can recommend me to other people. This isn't just a kid book assignment, it's my chance to do something else, something different, later on. This business is like being on probation your whole life. You're only as good as your last shoot, no matter who you are."

Jess rolled onto his shoulder, and her long hair tickled his neck. She didn't want her picture taken without permission. Kip knew it *was* a voyeuristic thing—photographing people when they didn't know it. He did it at sporting events or parks, experiments to catch faces, emotions. One reason he liked sports photography was that the athletes were so absorbed in what they were doing, they didn't stiffen up for the camera.

He wanted to capture that soft look Jess got when they made love, and he didn't know any way to do that. It's true, he made her look good, but that wasn't difficult. The camera liked her. The planes of her face reflected light. She looked better on film than in real life, where she scowled or frowned, where shadows showed under her chin and nose.

He could waste a brick on her face alone. He was afraid to ask her to pose nude. He wasn't sure he wanted to. And what would he do with the prints? He wasn't a fine arts photographer. He was a journalist, temporarily working for a book publisher.

For instance, right then Jess looked absorbed. She lay motionless, stared out the window. She was thinking about something. One day there would be two lines between her eyebrows, worry lines. The light was transparent outside, sunny, but indirect. How could he photograph her so that all of her was on film? Her intelligence? That lusty laugh? The hardheaded smarts, the vulnerable girl inside the defensive exterior?

He needed to make a hundred prints from a thousand exposures, and he didn't want to have to ask her permission each time. Other photographers could be reasonable and not use so much film and not get so absorbed and not get exhausted. But he didn't know any other way to be. He always went flat out, ninety miles an hour, as hard as he could. To get the best photographs he could.

# 6

*Kip's next trip took* him to a ranch in the southwestern part of the state, between Encampment and Saratoga. He stayed out four days waiting for pronghorn antelope and still didn't see one, although they were supposed to be thick in the country between sections of Medicine Bow National Forest. He did take photographs of the rancher and his son working cattle. Then he checked into a paper wall motel in Rock Springs and listened to eighteen-wheelers on Interstate 80 all night.

"You didn't have to kill yourself to get those shots printed up. You don't have to do that for money," Jess said.

"I can't let you support me."

"Why not? Have I asked for money? This is temporary. You'll get a check from New York."

"I owe money at the photo supply house."

"So what? I can afford it. This isn't some Victorian scenario."

"I feel bad if I don't pay my way."

"I don't want you to feel bad, but you look like warm death. You haven't slept since Thursday, and you look awful."

"I took pictures of the fire, then the people. Fires are tricky, the smoke confuses everything. I got a headache. Then after I got back here I took them in and printed them so the editor would have them this morning. I need some sleep." Kip rubbed three days' beard.

"Well, go sleep."

"Come talk to me."

"I'm all dressed to go out. We don't have anything to eat and I'm out of clean clothes."

"I'm too tired to mess you up, just lie down with me. I missed you more than I missed sleep."

Jess's anger dissolved and she kicked off her shoes. She led him into the bedroom as though he didn't know the way. She took off his shirt and pants. They lay on top of the blankets with his head in the crook of her arm. She smelled smoke in his hair, which he usually washed daily. On him was an onions-musk-male smell, plus the developer that clung to his hands.

"Want me to rub your back?"

"No, just talk. I need to hear you. One of the people died. They got everybody out, but this old man, I saw him coughing and hawking, and he was sitting up. Then later I saw this body covered and it was . . ." Kip's face convulsed, a spasm of pain, the witness's hard tears. He covered his face with his hands. She wrapped her arms around him, and he grabbed her tightly. She held him as he gasped. He lay motionless, waiting for the spasm to pass and when he turned away, her shirt was damp in front.

"Talk to me, anything, please."

"Well, I watched TV last night," she said, thinking how stupid she sounded, "but it wasn't any fun because you weren't here to hear all my smart remarks and snappy comebacks about "The Wild Wild West," which is full of anachronisms, or "Slattery." Then I started reading and fell asleep. Missing you. I have slept alone all my life, except for my blankie when I was little, and now I want you here. I don't miss it when I'm out—that's part of being in the field—just here." She almost added, "Where you belong."

She looked to see if he was asleep, but he grunted and she kept talking. She told him what Lewis and Clark had found when Sacajawea led them over the mountains with Baby Charbonneau on her back. In a few minutes his breathing was regular and his mouth fell open. She listened to his soft exhalations. It seemed unfair to watch him sleeping—like his taking her photograph when she didn't know it. Vulnerable time, trusting time.

A wave of affection overpowered her, and she couldn't breathe for a moment. She wanted to hold him like this and never let him be tired or hungry or ill. He was like a child who needed someone with some sense to make sure he took care of himself and kept a reasonable schedule.

One Friday when she had gotten home before he did, she looked out the window and saw him get out of his car. He left his cameras on the car seat and splashed through the mud puddles in the driveway with both feet, a grin on his face, just like a six-year-old.

Kip was a true artist, she decided. He didn't care about himself or how he appeared. He could act childish, like Picasso making a bull's head out of a bicycle seat.

Once he came back looking like a prisoner of war—gaunt, dehydrated, and hungry. She woke up in the morning and found him curled up in the middle of the floor.

"Why are you sleeping on the floor?" she asked.

"I'm so dirty, I didn't want to stink up the bed. And I was too tired to take a shower."

"I'll put coffee on."

When she came back, he had fallen asleep again. She got into the shower, shampooed her hair, took her time rinsing the long mop that hung halfway down her back. Then she heard him on the other side of the shower curtain.

"Do you mind?" he asked her.

"No, just don't flush, it'll scald me."

"Can I come in?"

"You're here."

"I mean in the shower."

"Sure."

She heard him strip off his clothes. He did truly stink—stale Kip and wood smoke from his campfire and weariness. Then he ducked inside the curtain and put his cold hands on her hips.

"You get under the shower," she said, and they shifted places. "Shall I do your hair?"

She massaged shampoo on his head. She loved to play with his hair, wet or dry. She did his back and he did hers, and then they started soaping personal places and giggling and pretty soon the hot water ran out, so they had to quit.

Afterward, she cut his hair "so he wouldn't be mistaken for a hippie." Shorthaired men—cowboys and oil workers and rednecks and state cops—had a nasty way of treating longhaired young men. Kip's hair was thick and very fine and stick straight. She trimmed a little at a time, afraid that her efforts would look amateurish. It was an excuse to have her hands in his soft hair.

That trip wasn't so bad. He recovered in a day. Usually that was all it took for him to bounce back. She felt cheated if she were home that day and he was sleeping, but she was afraid he'd get sick if he didn't take time off.

He kept "going on nerves," as her mother would put it. He pushed himself and never seemed to resent the drain, didn't even notice until he was finished. He concentrated like a little kid—totally absorbed in what he was doing. Sometimes Jess was utterly lost in her work and it felt good, but usually she was only too aware of what she needed to do and how long she had been working and how long it had been since she last ate and how soon she would quit.

Kip talked about nights he had spent in the photo lab at school, printing pictures, even when he wasn't supposed to be there. He'd been a stringer for AP his senior year, and he had an assignment from some USIA magazine to follow the head of the student council, Lon Gerald, for a year. He'd gone to classes with him, stayed with him in his fraternity house, gone out on dates with him—sometimes Lon would fix him up.

Kip had sat through student council meetings and gone back home to the farm where Lon and his father raised Charolais. He'd gone to Future Farmers of America meetings, because Gerald had also been involved in that organization. Gerald frankly couldn't wait to graduate from journalism school and ag school and get into politics. He was a good speaker, although Kip had gotten tired of sitting through the same speech over and over to student groups and farm groups. At graduation, instead of marching with his own graduating class, Kip had followed Lon Gerald.

He had done all this in addition to his regular class work and in addition to all the other photography he did for the newspaper. The only trouble, Kip ruefully confessed, was that he didn't make any money at all. He used to spend all that the magazine sent him on film. He needed a job where the magazine or newspaper would pay for it. He liked printing his own photographs because he wanted control. That part of the process took time, and that was another reason he spent long hours, sometimes days, immersed in that phase.

His time in the field had a different effect, Jess noticed. He would come back tired, hungry, and washed-out, but without the strain of the darkroom work or of staying on breaking news. He worked himself to a standstill. She was in the field, too, working twelve- and fourteen-hour days, but her work didn't drain her. She didn't overextend herself the way Kip did. Or maybe it was just the difference between their personalities.

When she got angry because he seemed stretched thin, she didn't know what to do. She had been raised to believe that she couldn't be bitchy, that she shouldn't complain. Anger was a sin. You were supposed to accept what your partner did, otherwise you were disloyal. She could hear her mother's voice in her head sometimes: "Never let the sun go down on your anger. If you can't say something nice, don't say anything at all." She consciously rejected her mother's attitudes, but they still lived in her memory.

When Kip was impatient with Jess, it drained her energy to keep on doing what she was doing and not give in to his demands. If she asked for changes, she felt like a nag. She was somehow supposed to make everything run smoothly for both parties without raising her voice or disturbing him. She was responsible for their happiness and well-being, but not supposed to exercise any power. That was crazy.

She was supposed to be content with her lot, even if she hadn't chosen it and didn't like it. Surely getting angry wouldn't destroy Kip. Surely he cared enough about her to do some of the things she wanted.

But he didn't think of them, and she didn't feel right asking him. And if she didn't ask, how was he to know? How was she supposed to keep from getting frustrated? She felt exploited, not by Kip, who was loving and understanding, but by the circumstances.

She worked as hard as he did, but only she felt responsible for housework. He would cook from time to time and seemed to enjoy it. He must have taken care of his own laundry at school and found something to eat. Why had it become her responsibility to wash his clothes and shop for groceries? Why had she assumed these were her jobs?

On the other hand, she wanted to take care of him. She wanted to feed him good food to keep him from getting even skinnier. Beef stew and vegetable soup and pork chops and gravy and fried chicken. She wanted him to feel cherished.

She wanted clean sheets for herself. She wanted the house clean, because she was more comfortable that way. When he did offer to help, she felt guilty if she took him up on it. Was she running him if she did? Was she being exploited if she didn't? If it became a problem, she could send out the laundry and hire a cleaning woman, although that seemed absurd for a furnished one-bedroom apartment.

Jess was trying to be a professional woman, trying to make her way in a demanding field, and she resented being sidetracked by trivial domestic problems. These things apparently never bothered Kip, although she didn't know if that was because he was male or because he was an artist.

So she told him how she felt, and he listened. Then he told her, and she listened, even if she didn't like what she heard. They didn't shake apart after all.

"What are you doing?" he asked.

"Listening." She lay with her ear to his chest, her hair trailing over his bare belly, still sweaty from their love-making.

"I think it's beating," he said and sighed, comfortable, relaxed.

"I don't know what a regular heartbeat sounds like, so I don't think I could hear the difference with your heart murmur. It sounds like a heart pumping—ka-thump, ka-thump."

"I don't think it's easy to hear. It was something the doctor found, but told me it didn't make any difference. But when it came time, it was good enough to keep me off the draft list."

Jess looked out the window. The sheer curtains filtered the bright June sunlight that afternoon. Corned beef and cabbage simmered on the stove. Kip had left laundry baskets full of clean, folded clothes on the big dresser. By the time they'd gotten to the laundromat they'd needed eight washers and a lot of bleach and borax. They had had two loads of jeans alone.

His heart beat steady as a drummer. The faulty valve didn't slow it down. She imagined the red, slippery heart from science class movies. It contracted and relaxed, pumping inside its transparent sac like a fist clenching and unclenching. She wondered if the muscles making diastole *shuush* and systole *numph* faltered or tired. His heart pounded faster and faster when they coupled, then soon slowed to normal, no worse from the exertion. Smoking didn't seem to affect it. If he had a problem, surely it would have shown up after one of his marathon trips backpacking into the mountains.

Thinking about his heart murmur was a way of avoiding other murmurs: I love you. I care about you. It's your turn to take out the trash. Where are my sweat socks? Talk to me, I missed your voice. Do you have the sports section? I love it when you do that. You're beautiful.

They tried to work out the anger they were afraid of. What they had was too provisional. If they knew it would be forever and ever, they could risk rocking the boat. *Till death do us part* would give time enough to mend damage. They were terribly civilized and restrained when they disagreed, like bad actors in a play.

Could discord enter the atrium, invade the auricle, rush the lungs? Be expelled as a breath of hate? Would sorrow blacken the connective endothelial tissue? Would pain arrest the muscles' push and keep the valve from closing? Would fury obstruct the aorta, clamp off the flow of blood? She was glad that his heart murmured.

"I hate to think of you in Vietnam," she said, "getting shot at."

"I wouldn't mind going as a photographer, but when you're a soldier, you can't quit and go back to Saigon and take your film to the lab."

"Would you have gone to Canada?"

"I don't know. I thought about it. Sometimes I feel unpatriotic because I had a legal way out. But the ones that are coming back make it sound like a real hellhole, with nobody knowing what's going on. Robert Capa, the *Life* photographer, got killed when he stepped on a land mine in 1954. What's the point?"

# 7

*They spent a week in* Yellowstone in July, backpacking in the wilderness. Jess loved it there, away from people, away from phones and cars and newspapers. When she went back to work, she lived on memories: the ten-thousand-foot dawns, the hikes that made them wheeze until they got enough oxygen, the nights they spent zipped together in their sleeping bags.

Kip filled in the species missing from Sarah's list. He found a rancher in the grasslands in the Southwest who had wild mustangs, but Sarah wasn't interested in them. He would stay in Wyoming for the elk rut at the national refuge near Jackson in November.

"Last winter, I made every mistake. The oil in the cameras froze up, the film broke until I learned to keep my cameras inside my parka. My fat-man parka."

"This year, you'll be ready. That shaving brush hanging on your coat looks like the tail of some strange animal, like you've got a ferret in your pocket."

"Without oil that camera is going to die an early death."

"It's in a good cause." Jess kissed him and sent him out. He looked like an arctic explorer. All he needed were sled dogs.

When it happened, it came together all at once. The woman, her husband, the obstetrician, and the hospital all agreed to let Kip do a photo essay on the delivery of a baby. Jess went to the hospital with him, but the doctors wouldn't let her in the delivery room. "But I've done this before," she wanted to tell them. She helped Kip write the captions, and the Casper editor gave it two full pages. They celebrated with steak and champagne.

The state tourism people bought a selection of his prints, including portraits and some of the water-snow photographs from the mountains and grassland photos from the eastern part of the state. They refused photos of the Tetons-Jackson-Yellowstone area—overphotographed, Kip guessed.

He had paid Jess back and his checking account was fat when he got a phone call from Sarah Brocklein to come to New York. He took a portfolio filled with photos and slides with him and planned to see as many magazine photo editors as he could.

Sarah Brocklein praised his animal photos and promised to recommend him.

While he was in New York, *Life* bought the childbirth photo essay from the Casper newspaper and asked to see more, so Jess relayed the message and Kip went to the Time-Life Building on Sixth Avenue for an interview.

Jess knew what was coming before she drove to Denver to pick him up.

"Come to New York with me."

They sat at the chrome and red Formica dining table. A pot of soup warmed on the stove. Kip was high, excited, happy. They had beaten a winter storm coming home, and the first gray flakes flew around the windows now. Gray skies lowered over the winter landscape frozen hard as iron, waiting for the snow.

"What would I do in New York? Sit in an apartment while you're out on assignment?"

"I'll be based there, doing local news for a while, stuff nobody else wants to do."

"I can't do hydrology in New York City."

"I can't give up this chance."

"I wouldn't want you to." The words came out right, but she knew she didn't mean them. "I don't want to blow my chance here in Wyoming, with the Survey, doing what I'm trained to do." Doing what I love, she added to herself.

"Is there anything I can say that would make you change your mind?" Kip sounded almost frantic.

"No." Tears ran down Jess's face, and she got up to grab a paper towel to wipe her nose.

"How about, 'Marry me'?"

Jess stopped. The thing they had never talked about. She wanted it—as tribute, and because she wanted him, and because he cared about her. But not seriously, because then she'd have to make a decision.

"What?" She had heard, but she couldn't take it in.

"Marry me." Kip's face lit up in a wide, high-energy grin.

Then Jess really broke down and cried. Kip put his arms around her. "Does this mean you're happy?"

Her chest heaved and her back was tense and the sobs convulsive.

"What kind of an answer is that?" he murmured as he stroked her hair away from her cheek.

"Can't," Jess gasped.

She gradually calmed down. Kip turned off the fire under the soup and poured glasses of the wine she had opened for dinner. He chugged his and she took a few sips and after a while she could breathe.

"I can't give up what I'm working for here," she said. The tears began again, softly this time. "I don't want to. I want to stay with you, but this was coming all along whether we knew it or not."

"Do you want to marry me?" he asked.

"Sometimes. I haven't let myself think it."

"Do you want me to stay here?" he asked.

"You're not serious."

"Say I was."

"You'd stay here, get a job, and hate me forever because I kept you from finding out if you were really, really good."

Kip hung his head and nodded. "You're probably right." They sat there, each with his own thoughts for a while.

"I feel like I owe you something," Kip said. "I've taken and taken and taken all you gave and I haven't given you much in return."

"I wasn't keeping book."

"You know what I mean."

She shrugged.

"You let me move in here, and if I hadn't had a place to stay it would have been really hard when I ran out of money. And you took care of me when I came in tired. You cared about what I was doing, about me. And we . . . played a lot together."

"That was the best part—playing. You gave, too. All the things you shared. Soap bubbles." She was trying to be generous and not let self pity make this worse. "You lighten me up."

"You gave me your best."

"The best I had left after work," Jess corrected. The astringent truth cut through the sentimentality.

"I guess we both did, but it wasn't fifty-fifty, and I want you to know I realize I took more than I gave."

"I didn't do anything I didn't want to. I always felt I was holding a little of myself back because it would hurt too much when it was over if I gave everything. It didn't work." She tried to smile, but her face crumpled again. Kip reached for her, but she shook her head.

"I won't go with you. You won't stay. I guess we need to get out of this as cleanly as we can."

Jess didn't know she could feel so bad and still stand up. "I'm not hungry, but help yourself." She put her wineglass in the sink and went into the bedroom. She closed the door, lay down on the bed, kicked her shoes off, and stared at the ceiling.

Kip said through the door: "If there was any way of doing this without hurting you, I'd do it."

Tears ran into her hair and ears, and she wiped them on the pillowcase.

The first months in New York were a blur for Kip. He found an apartment, not rent-controlled but cheap enough. He bought a mattress, then picked up the rest of his furniture from the street on trash day. He worked doggedly photographing a tuna can, or a VIP, whatever *Life* editors gave him, and after a while, he started getting better assignments.

He must have bought clothes, groceries, gone to movies and galleries, but his memory of that time was vague. He felt guilty because he rarely thought of Jess. He still loved her, but there was too much going on in his life.

Then he got an assignment on drug addicts, followed them around for weeks, was even mistaken for one. A cop tried to bust him, didn't believe his *Life* credentials, thought he'd stolen the cameras. He got some shots he didn't think would turn out, but they did, of dope deals on street corners at night. Anybody can take pictures when the sun shines. The photos and the written essay took him and the writer to Kentucky to the addicts' hospital, and the magazine ran the story and photos in two issues. He got a byline credit, not just six-point type in the photo credits.

After Kip left, November was an endless stretch of miserable days and desolate nights for Jess. There were a few seconds of peace each morning when she woke up, and then she would remember—as she reached for the alarm, or walked to the bathroom, or pulled on her robe—that Kip was gone. She could scarcely drag herself to work but would stay late until her eyes wouldn't focus in order to put off going home to the empty apartment. Her work, which was so important, didn't fill the gap Kip left.

She phoned her parents on Thanksgiving Day, grateful for their constant support, then went to dinner at the home of one of the young married geologists, Paul

Storms, whose wife, Mil, had cooked a huge and elaborate dinner.

The men seemed guarded, and the wives distant. Jess knew they resented her because she worked with their husbands. She talked shop with the men, then helped serve the sweet potatoes and green beans. She filled in when the hostess left to tend Jonathan, their two-year-old. The women warmed up to her a bit, and by the time they washed dishes, things felt a little better. Jess wished she had a baby, like Mil, anything to fill the empty place. Until Kip had shown up, she hadn't known she was missing anything.

The dispenser with the last of the birth control pills hit the wastebasket with a clatter. She stripped the windows of curtains, the bed of the spread, the couch of its cover. She rolled up the throw rugs and took them all to the laundromat. She cleaned like a dervish—washed windows, scrubbed cabinets, wiped out drawers.

She kept finding traces of Kip—photo magazines in the stack beside the couch, shaving cream in the medicine chest. She tried to get rid of all traces of him because it hurt so much to find them. When the apartment was immaculate, she went to *The Sound of Music*, which she didn't like much, and cried from "Climb Every Mountain" until theTrapp children's glockenspiel song, then she gathered up used tissues and walked out. She did this five times.

She drove up Casper Mountain and walked the winter trails, bleak and worn from summer's use. She went back every weekend until she knew them by heart and the windchill was too cold to bear.

She forwarded his phone calls to the photo desk at *Life* magazine, but didn't try to reach Kip herself. She didn't want to weep over the phone.

She grinched-out, lied to her parents, said she couldn't get home for Christmas. She thought of the Plaza lights in Kansas City and all the familiar holiday routines, but she knew her depression showed, and she didn't want to face her mother's inquisition. Or worse, her parents' sympathy, which would destroy her.

After the first high-energy months on the job, Jess hit a slump. She made a couple of mistakes that made her feel vulnerable and unsure of herself and of what her coworkers thought of her. She went to a couple of parties in Casper and met new people, traveled to Cheyenne for meetings on a project in Yellowstone, and noticed more single men she worked with.

Then, one morning just before Christmas, it struck her that it was 10 A.M. before she thought of Kip.

Christmas Eve she stayed at the office to clean up her desk and keep from getting behind in her project work. Why even try to get any work done between Christmas and New Year's? Most of the office was on use-or-lose vacation time.

A man wandered into the office with a long white florist's box and was directed to her desk. A dozen red roses rested in a cloud of fern, wrapped in green tissue paper. The card read: "There's an envelope taped to the underside of the bottom drawer of your dresser. Love—Kip." She had to take a lot of teasing from the guys at lunch.

She stopped at Osco on the way home to buy a vase. No one had ever given her florist flowers before. She put the roses—too perfect, too beautiful—in the middle of the kitchen table, then pulled out the dresser drawer. Masking tape held a big manila envelope in place. She took the drawer out and carefully peeled away the tape.

Inside were photographs and a letter that was dated before he left.

> Jess—
>
> This is "my best"—not much, but maybe they'll bring back good memories.
>
> Love—
>
> Kip

One by one, she studied the photos. Some were on glossy paper, as he prepared them for publication. A few still had captions taped on. Some were on matte paper:

Barely discernible people clustered around the pot-bellied stove at the Valverde Hotel in Socorro, New Mexico.

A close-up of a coney—the epitome of cute, cuter than chipmunks.

Two people skiing across a mountain park of fresh powder.

An exhausted firefighter, his face blackened from smoke.

Two men in ranch garb—one older, one younger, looking at a downed heifer with worried eyes.

A cloud of steam floating above hot springs where the water ran into a cold creek. Ice on the bare cottonwood branches hanging over the creek. An elk feeding in the background.

Jess recognized the ones that had run in the Casper paper. Kip had reprinted some on heavy stock:

The jubilant face of the woman as the doctor showed her the infant she had just delivered.

From the rodeo at the end of July, the steer wrestler in midair, reaching for the horns of the wild-eyed steer.

And at the bottom of the stack she found three

photographs of herself, taken with permission one weekend. They didn't look stiff or posed. In one she is reading, her face absorbed, serious. In the second she is outdoors, laughing, her head tipped back, her hair flying. In the last she is simply smiling into the camera. Her eyes are full of love. She flushed when she remembered that shot and how he kept cranking and shooting until she made love to him and he had to stop. She looked beautiful.

Tears rolled down her face. He had signed them all.

He had photographed her with love, as he did all his subjects.

New Year's Day the phone rang as she lay, torpid, in front of the TV.

"I didn't want to make you cry," Kip said, explaining why he hadn't phoned before.

"Maybe I can talk without crying now," Jess said.

He gave her his phone number and told her about the assignments he'd done and dropped the names of some of the people he had met.

She told him about moving up two grades after a year and the new wells she would put in and it was okay, really okay. And she loved the pictures he left.

They were good friends and they could talk and remember things they'd done. He missed the clean air and open spaces and she wanted to know how exciting the city was. He was fine and she said she would be okay eventually and they were both glad they'd been together.

# 8

*In October 1968*, when Toby was six weeks old, Jess accompanied Karl to Santa Fe where he would attend a business conference. When Jess saw Kip across the lobby, she almost dropped her baby.

"What is it?" Karl asked, looking up from suitcases and baby paraphernalia.

"Sean Kilpatrick—my photographer-friend Kip."

"What's he doing in Santa Fe?"

"How should I know? I haven't seen him in three years."

La Fonda, the oldest hotel in Santa Fe, was a relic of the days when hotels with Southwestern architecture and decor were the pride of the Atchison, Topeka, and Santa Fe Railroad. A large restaurant adjoined the patio, and shops lined the first floor indoors and out. It was comfortable and central to the plaza and to Karl's conference.

Jess's knees felt funny as she walked across the crowded lobby to the desk. She felt the weight of Toby in her arms, squirming but not yet fussing.

"Kip?"

He looked up and took several seconds before he registered who she was. He looked ten years older, not three, skinnier than she thought possible, and utterly exhausted. He was shorthaired and clean-shaven, but he looked like he'd just come in from a weekend in Needle Park. His eyes seemed to sink into his skull, and his neck bent under the weight of cameras.

"Jess?"

She nodded and laughed, and Kip smiled and looked down at the baby.

"Meet Toby the Wonder Child, six weeks old tomorrow."

Kip studied the baby, who returned his gaze. He stuck out a forefinger and Toby curled dimpled fingers around it and pulled it toward her mouth. They played tug-of-war for a few moments.

"This is my husband, Karl Stefan," Jess said. The men shook hands.

"Didn't expect, I mean, this is a . . ." Kip ducked his head.

Jess put a hand on his sleeve. "Will you be here long?"

"I'm meeting a writer who's flying out from New York. I have to pick him up in Albuquerque day after tomorrow."

"Are you free for dinner tonight?" Jess looked at Karl, who shrugged and nodded.

"Sure," said Kip. He rested his thin hand on Toby's head.

Kip didn't show up at Jaramillo's restaurant in Chimayo at seven, as agreed. At seven-thirty he still wasn't there.

"What's keeping him?" Karl complained. He ordered another Bloody Mary.

"I don't know. I gave him our room number. He could have called."

"Beats me what you saw in him," Karl muttered, running his hands through his thick blond hair.

"He isn't as beautiful as you," said Jess, smiling. She longed to comfort her husband.

"He doesn't look healthy."

"Probably too many assignments back to back."

She wondered if Kip was smoking or drinking too much or just working too hard. She felt fat and sloppy in comparison. She still had a few extra pounds since Toby was born, and her breasts seemed enormous, swollen with milk. Karl liked to taste her breasts, and they ached when she thought of making love with him.

She had told Karl that she had lived with the photographer, that it was over, and that she had no regrets. Karl had promised never to question her about Kip, but she could see him wrestling with the temptation now.

"Why don't we go ahead and order?" she suggested. Toby, propped up in the Infanseat, stared at the people and the waiters and dropped her pacifier and charmed the maitre d'. They ate the spicy northern New Mexico food, with the green chile salsa Jess loved, and left when Toby started to fuss.

Jess wondered why Kip had stood them up. The next morning she left a message at the desk and spent an hour with Toby wandering in and out of the shops on the plaza. When she went back to their room to put Toby down for a nap, the message light was blinking.

The desk clerk read: "Sorry about dinner. Try again?" and a room number.

Before she could phone, Karl came in from the morning's session.

"I'm going for a drink with some of the people from the conference. I'll eat lunch with them. I can't sit through the afternoon meetings without a drink."

"I was going to have lunch with Kip," Jess said. "I want you to keep Toby."

Karl scowled.

"What's the matter?" she asked.

"Nothing. I'll be back in half an hour and you can leave then."

So Jess phoned Kip and arranged to meet him in the hotel restaurant, but Karl didn't get back in time, so she packed up Toby, whom she had just nursed, and pushed the stroller down to the lobby, thoroughly ticked at Karl.

Her bad temper evaporated when she saw Kip.

"Beautiful," said Kip, smiling. He reached for Toby. The little girl allowed herself to be cuddled against Kip's thin chest. He even took off a camera.

"Karl was supposed to baby-sit," she began.

"That's all right." He rested Toby on his bony knee. "I'm sorry about last night. I had a couple of drinks and at this altitude, they wiped me out. I thought I'd wake up in time."

It was awkward to carry on a conversation. She wanted to ask him why he looked so bad and did he have a girlfriend and was she pretty, did he still like New York and how was work going. Instead Jess asked about his assignment, and he told her he planned to go to Nevada to photograph wild horses, who were endangered.

"I know a rancher in Wyoming who has wild mustangs on his ranch," he said.

"Is that the same one you found before? Sarah didn't want those horses."

"Well, I'm getting another chance. Trying to catch their movement on film, with a still camera."

"Have you thought of movies or video?"

He shook his head. "It'll take me the rest of my life to get good with a Leica."

She told him about Toby and explained why they were in Santa Fe. "Karl said why drill for oil, spend a million dollars to sink a well, when you can make as much money building houses and hotels? It's supposed to work unless you run into zoning laws or opposition from local hotshots. This meeting is on New Mexico laws, very complicated here, Indian pueblos and Spanish land grants. I'm just a simple geologist. I leave business to Karl. He may decide it's easier in Wyoming."

"How'd you meet him?" Kip asked. He scarcely looked at her but was fascinated with Toby, who chewed on his shirt and spat up on his lap.

"He was with an oil company that wanted to drill, and there's a lot of paperwork before you get the permit. I got involved because my agency is interested in what will happen to underground water. I wrote the report. We got to know each other."

"He's an asshole."

"Thanks a lot."

"Hell, so am I," said Kip. "There's a lot of that going around."

"What's wrong?" Jess asked after they ate. "You look tired."

"I am tired. And I can't get off the merry-go-round."

"I saw the assassination pictures. That must have been hard."

Kip grunted.

Jess wondered if the ghosts still claimed him. "What was it like, before it happened?"

He gave her a funny look and cleared his throat. He didn't say anything for a long moment, then seemed to make a decision.

"We had been on the road for months, and all the reporters and photographers were like a family. 'On to Chicago!' we said. Everybody was high because he'd won California. My editors thought he'd be the next president and told me to stick close to him.

"I had one camera around my neck and one under my jacket—a couple of Nikkormats—along with a spare lens in my pocket. I had three rolls of film. Downstairs, we walked through the hotel kitchen, and Kennedy went to speak to the crowd in the ballroom. When he finished and came off the stage, his bodyguard said, 'Senator, we're going this way,' But Kennedy said no and pointed back toward the kitchen. He wasn't supposed to walk into the kitchen like that—I was about ten feet behind him— I heard shots."

Kip's face convulsed. He bent over Toby and put her in her stroller so Jess couldn't see his face. No sound, no tears. He held his breath, waited, then gasped when he exhaled. "Sorry."

"Go ahead," said Jess. "Get it out."

"There was this radio guy asking questions as we walked into the kitchen. Kennedy was shaking hands with the kitchen workers. The photographers usually formed a wedge that got us close enough for pictures. Only that time, he had changed directions, abruptly. We scrambled to reform the wedge, but we were all behind him. I heard shots—I knew it was gunfire. People diving, shots and screams. I dove. I didn't know who was hit.

"The radio guy just kept talking into his mike. 'Grab him, Rafer! Get the gun. Grab it.' People shouting. Paul was bleeding. Two steps further, I came upon the senator. I looked at the scene and said, 'This is wrong,' so I ran to the senator's feet. The radio guy was shouting, 'He's pointing it. Break his thumb!' Then, quieter, 'Kennedy has been shot.' People all over and I kept trying for a shot." Kip's eyes were wet.

"Conditioned response," Jess said. "Dogs salivate; you take pictures."

"The TV cameraman froze. His lighting technician pushed the button and told him to shoot and he pointed the camera until the film ran out." Kip absently stroked Toby's head as he talked.

"When I ran around the body to the feet, people were everywhere, the scene was blocked, but it opened up for a second. There was just the TV light and some fluorescents. I didn't know what the exposure was. I had time to shoot just four frames, bracketed. The film was pushed two stops. The first frame was out of focus, the next a little more in focus. The third frame was the one with the busboy looking up.

"All this going through my head instead of thinking of a man dying. We didn't know he was dying, he was still breathing then. Bedlam. Ethel wanted all the photographers out of the room. Because they knew me, I wasn't thrown out. I backed up and put my arms out to hold back the crowd. But every once in a while I'd reach down and take a picture. I didn't know what I had. The guy in the lab really got the picture—Kennedy on the floor, the busboy looking up."

They sat in silence for a while.

"It must have been horrible for you," said Jess.

Once Kip started talking, he rambled on. They got up

and pushed the stroller outside. He talked, compulsively now, about the bus and Sylvia, who was the *Life* reporter, and the speech and George Bernard Shaw quotes and the damned dog in Indiana. The media people lived with Kennedy, receiving each morning a piece of paper telling what the senator and they would do that day. Seven days a week, for months, all over the country, one primary after another, sharing everything, living in the mother plane, Kennedy with them in the plane, friendly—singing, talking.

"They ran my photo on the cover—Kennedy in the surf with the dog." Kip shook his head and said he didn't know if the country could survive if they kept killing off the best people. Kennedy had been a shoo-in for Chicago, then McCarthy caved in. He wanted to cover the convention in Chicago, but *Life* already had several photographers assigned. It looked like Nixon was going to whip Humphrey next month.

Jess was ashamed that she hadn't been following the news and didn't understand all the references Kip made, but it was only important to nod and say, "Mhmm, yes," and keep pushing the stroller.

"I'm not doing any more political stuff for a while. It's all smoke and mirrors and images. The reporters and the sources are too close."

They stopped at the Woolworth's on the plaza, and Kip bought a bottle of soap bubbles and blew them. Toby watched, fascinated.

Jess loved the buildings, low and clustered, their scale personal, not monumental. She had read the history and now she was walking the streets. She planned to buy a rug at one of the shops around the plaza. Indians spread out their jewelry under the Palace of the Governors *portale*. She pushed the stroller along the sidewalks, and then they sat for a few moments on a bench, but quickly got cold. She checked to see if Toby was warm enough in the fleece bunting.

"Do you want to see the cathedral?" Jess asked. "The one from Willa Cather's novel?"

Kip looked blank.

"Well, I do."

They walked up San Francisco Street to the church, and Kip lifted the stroller up the steps to the churchyard. Jess looked up at the curious Hebrew characters in stained glass over the main door. "The archbishop built the wrong church," she said.

Evidently Kip had not read the story.

"He got workmen to build in the French style, of the province where he grew up," Jess explained. "He even found that golden limestone, which is rare around here. And he built this cold, lovely building, completely different from the rest of the town. It should have been built of mud." She looked from the churchyard down the streets of ocher adobe, with the umber desert stretching west to carnelian mountains.

"We all build the wrong buildings," Kip said.

"Please."

"We choose the wrong profession, we marry the wrong people."

"Don't, please."

"I'm jealous of your marriage, of your baby."

"Be jealous. I envy your excitement, all the traveling, all the interesting things you do."

"I wonder what your husband envies."

"Your freedom, no doubt," said Jess.

"How did you get together?"

"We were in meetings together, working on the permit. We started buzzing around each other. He's very kind and stubborn and affectionate, although in public he sometimes acts like a macho big shot."

"You found the boy inside."

"I found a man. His family has a ranch. They're not rich, but they're good people. I love his mother. We went with all his cousins and uncles and aunts for their annual family reunion last summer at Moose Lake. And I wasn't getting any younger."

"You're what? Twenty-eight?"

"More. And my parents were relieved and happy, although of course my Dad said Karl wasn't good enough for me and my mother just smiled and said, 'Nobody would be.' She always wanted me to be self-reliant, then when I was, she was afraid I'd scare all the men away."

"And it's all working out."

"He travels and I'll stay in Cheyenne. I've transferred to the office there. Kids need to go to school in one place."

"More kids?"

"Probably. I'd hate to get all this good experience and never put it to use again." She looked at him and wished she could erase the dark circles under his eyes and feed him vegetables and beef stew and potatoes. "Will you get married?" she asked.

"Someday, when I find the right girl. God, the last one wasn't the right one. But someday."

"Good. If I can't take care of you, I want you to find someone who will. You don't do drugs, do you? That's all we hear about New York."

"I photograph junkies, that's all."

They went inside the big church.

# 9

*The Virgin's altar drew Kip* with its warmth. In an alcove on the left side, at the front of the church near the main altar, hundreds of candles burned before an ornately dressed madonna. The area was noticeably brighter and warmer. Crutches, photographs, and letters littered the area in front of the little side altar. Other images of the Virgin decorated the walls. To Kip the rest of the church felt formal, tasteful, empty.

He tried an available light photograph, using the candlelight, but the madonna was just a Spanish doll. Then he tried the Leica, one-thirtieth of a second, f 2.8.

"Come here," he said. "Take Toby out of that thing." He draped one of the baby's blankets over Jess's head. Her long, straight brown hair, parted in the middle, looked immediately peasant. Kip shot her and Toby with their faces illuminated from below by the banked rows of votive candles in their red glass holders. Then he moved the candle stand and the metal scraped across the stone floor.

"You can't do that!" Jess said, but Kip squeezed through the space he made.

"Are you going to climb up the altar?" Jess asked.

He shot them from the front, then nearly knocked a lamp over, so he came out where Jess knelt.

An old woman hobbled into the area on arthritic feet, and Kip turned his camera on her. After a few shots he asked if she minded. She shrugged and turned her back on him. He wished he had someone to hold a reflector and just a little more light. He wanted her wrinkle-eroded face as she murmured her devotions.

"Hasn't this been done?" asked Jess. She pulled the blanket off her head and jiggled Toby to quiet her.

"Probably, but this is the first time since June I've taken a photograph I wasn't paid to take."

"That's a good sign. I need to get back and feed Toby."

"Didn't you bring a bottle?"

"That's not how I feed her."

"Then you don't need to go back yet."

"I do need to sit down, and I feel uncomfortable talking in church."

They found a restaurant nearby and ordered coffee in the midafternoon lull. Southwest decor, relentless terra cotta pots and Indian-style blankets. The waitress made a fresh pot of coffee, and Kip ate a piece of blueberry pie. Jess arranged the baby blanket over one shoulder and with her back to the restaurant, tucked Toby underneath and unbuttoned her blouse. Kip wanted to stare. He wanted to know what this was like, how it felt. He wanted to photograph it.

"You can watch," said Jess. "You've seen my tits before." Then she bit her lip. They had made no references to the old days or what they had done. Toby was their chaperone and they resolutely spoke of everything else.

"I never saw them being put to that use before," he said.

"Do you think Karl is jealous of you?" Jess asked.

"Sure."

"But he's the one I married."

"Did you tell him about us?"

"I said we lived together and it was over and he promised never to bring it up."

"Throw it up to you, you mean."

"Something like that."

"He's jealous because we still love each other."

"Do we?" She looked down at Toby's hand kneading her breast. She raised the baby for a burp, then changed to the other side.

"We love each other like friends," she amended.

"No. Like lovers."

"We're not," said Jess.

"But we're inside each other's heads, thinking together, the way we always did. I can almost feel that baby on me. I almost know the weight of your love for her. It fills you now, you're absorbed. You sensed how rotten I felt and you let me talk. You're the only person who has ever seen me cry. And Karl can't share that."

"How did you learn so much? From meeting him for a minute last night? Don't spoil this."

"I see myself in him. He's jealous because we slept together, he doesn't like that, but he's even more jealous that we shared intimacy that's closer than sex."

The coffee hit Kip's stomach and he pulled a roll of antacid tablets out of his pocket and stuck one in his mouth. All his nerve endings were hypersensitive, and he felt the lack of oxygen in the seven-thousand-foot air and the clarity of the autumn light, the piñon pine smoke in the air. He felt the baby's tug on Jess's nipple.

"You can't keep going like this," said Jess. "You'll get sick."

"I'm already sick. Ulcer."

"What are you going to do?"

"I can't quit *Life*—once you've been there, everything else is down."

"Can you change your focus? Try something new?"

"That's why I'm here. Jackson and I are going after mustangs. Co Rentmeester, also on staff, is doing endangered species, critter pictures that remind me of my Wyoming animals. Every time I get out West, more things have disappeared. I want to record some of them. I wish I could live here and work in New York. Right now I need to get away from the city."

"You could always get a desk job, couldn't you?"

He raised his eyebrows in a "get serious" expression.

"I just don't want you sick," she said. Kip sank into silence, drank water, and chewed another tablet.

Jess burped Toby and put her back under the blanket.

"Tell me about Karl, make him real so I know him as a person and he's not just this Nordic barbarian who stole you away."

"I went willingly," Jess said. "Why do you want to know about him?"

"If I know him and he's a real person and my friend, then I have to leave you alone. I couldn't hurt a friend."

"I guess that makes sense." Jess gave her head a shake. "He went to Colorado State, Fort Collins, and he started out managing his parents' ranch, near Rawlings. Then his father died and he decided he didn't want to keep doing that. So he tried the oil business, working for a big company. He wanted to be his own boss, but that takes *mucho dinero* capital. Right now he's making a living and his younger brother manages the ranch. Karl thinks this real estate promotion will make us rich. I just hope it makes him happy. I'm going back to the Survey in a couple of weeks."

"Would you rather stay home with the baby?" Kip asked.

"Sure. It would be easy to melt into the wife-and-mommy role."

"What's wrong with the role?"

Toby relaxed. Kip saw her mouth fall away from the nipple. Jess handed him the baby and moistened a napkin in her water glass and wiped Toby's face. Then she buttoned herself up.

"I need to know I'm competent at something," Jess said, "that I can be a professional person. I worked so hard to get the Survey to take me seriously, I can't just give it all up and let Karl support me. They didn't like it when I was out in the field pregnant, so someone always came with me. I kept working until I went into labor, just to prove that women could have children and still do the job. Now I'm going back. Besides, we don't know if this subdivision idea will work."

"Most women used to stay home if they could."

"I've got some weird insecurity, I don't know where it comes from, that I can't depend on someone else. My mother and my father were married, then he went off and got killed in the Battle of the Bulge and all the time when I was little, mother worked. After she married Daddy, the only father I know, she always insisted I had to be self-reliant."

"Which you are. You don't have to prove anything."

"Yes, I do. I have to prove that a woman can be a wife

and mother and a professional geologist, too. But I get so tired," she said. Tears filled her eyes. "I get tired of fighting all the time, to make them understand. I had to teach Karl and his brother and his uncles. I am such an oddity. And the women in his family were kind, but they didn't support me. They just let the men walk all over them. They don't know it could be any different. It's hard. I love Karl—yes, I can love two men at the same time. He is good for me. He's a wonderful person. He just isn't as liberated as I am. And I don't want to cave in now after I've worked so hard."

Kip waited, then said: "I never understood what you were up against. I didn't treat you in a very liberated way."

"You were fine." Jess blotted her face with her napkin.

"You're *supposed* to fall into roles when you have kids. I'm sure Karl is a decent guy. You and Karl aren't hippies, living in the woods, eating alfalfa sprouts."

Jess smiled.

"You two want to do the right thing, make a marriage together, take care of the kid. It's going to turn you into different people."

"I know. It has already. He's gentler, I'm more patient. I don't *have* to go to work to survive, Karl makes money and the family has money—actually property. I have to go back to work because I'm afraid I'll turn into a nothing. I'll keep doing what I think he wants and trying to be what he wants until I won't have anything of myself left. I'll be the little woman."

"Do you want to go back to the hotel?" asked Kip.

"Yes. No." She drank more coffee and seemed distracted.

Her lipstick was gone and her hair was tangled around her face. He remembered kissing that face, feeling that hair brush his skin.

"You're bringing up things I haven't thought about," she said. "I really want to get back to work, doing something I love, in spite of paperwork and office politics and always wishing for more sleep. But I'll miss this time with Toby. I'd like to think she needs me twenty-four hours a day, but I know better."

"You never needed me." Kip felt bitter and alone and he knew he sounded self-pitying. "You could always take care of yourself."

"I need to know that you're somewhere in the world, that you still love me some way or another. We aren't going to change. I don't want you to rescue me from married life. I never wanted to force you to stay. But it means something to know you care about me, when I'm tired and bogged down in the repetitious, ordinary parts of my life." She looked at him and murmured, almost inaudibly, "Think of me sometimes."

He nodded and felt choked up.

"I always thought if I had found the magic words, you would have come with me," he said. "To New York."

Jess smiled. "I always thought you'd come back. You have, just not the way I imagined three years ago."

Then he said, "You stroke this baby, feed her, bathe her, talk to her. Carry her around, love her." He thought for a moment, looked down on the pulse beating in the fontanel. "I was reading Reich, how we store emotions in our bodies. His ideas were about pain—old injuries, psychological trauma—stored in muscles, lungs, hearts. He invented therapy to cure people who armor themselves against the world." He rested his hand on Toby's head and continued: "So if we can store negative stuff, emotional pain, physical damage, why can't we store love? Toby has all this experience of you caring for her. It's bound to help her grow up."

"That's beautiful," said Jess.

"And we store in our cells, our muscles, our bones, in all the wet tissues, all the secret places—love, joy, delight. Pleasure. Caring. Do you remember giving me showers, practically hand-feeding me, tucking me in?"

Jess nodded. "You were my baby then."

"Don't you think my body has stored all that caring? Don't you think it helps me?"

She couldn't talk.

Finally, he said, "There's always something in our way."

Kip carried the sleeping Toby and Jess pushed the laden stroller back to La Fonda. They stood at the elevators.

"I'm leaving early in the morning to pick up Jackson," said Kip.

"Give something back," said Jess. It was an intuitive leap.

"What?"

"You *take* pictures, you *shoot* people, you give back images, prints. You need to give back something more."

"How did you know about that?" he asked.

"About what?" Jess took Toby.

"I got asked to go back to M.U., to journalism school, to do a workshop—young photographers spend a week in some Missouri town and do saturation coverage. I said no, I wasn't good enough. I can't judge anybody else's work. I was really afraid I couldn't teach them anything."

"Next time they ask you, do it. You could see Cliff Edom, and give back something. Not because the workshop needs you. You need it."

Kip nodded. "I'm glad I got to see you one more time."

He put his arms around her and they embraced, the baby between them. She bent her head toward his and their foreheads touched.

# 10

Christmas 1968

Well, Kip, I went back to work after I saw you in Santa Fe. I took Toby with me to a training course. Nobody had ever heard of such a thing! Everybody in Karl's family expected me to quit working, then not only did I go back to work, but I took Toby. I decided I could find a baby-sitter in Jackson as easily as Cheyenne. I didn't want to leave her for a week. Every morning I expressed my milk and took it and Toby to the sitter and went to my meetings. At the end of the day I picked Toby up, fed her, ate, and played with her. I'm in the field a lot, but when I get home to Cheyenne Karl and I try to make up for all the time apart. Karl is in Laramie most of the time working on this subdivision. He's doing it by the book and it looks like it's going to work.

I see the snow differently, I see the mountains differently since I've seen your photos. I have some wildlife friends and they see more than I do when we're out hiking—they know what to watch for. Your photos are like that: I notice more. Thanks for the prints, which are at the frame shop.

Love—
Jess

**Merry Christmas and Happy New Year—1970**

In California, Santa Claus wears a designer T-shirt. I'm living in Lotusland, but at least I can drive into the mountains when I'm finished.

Love—Kip

Christmas 1971

Kip, this has been a rough year for all of us. Karl's mother, Alice, died in November and Karl, who never paid much attention to her when she was alive, went all to pieces after the funeral.

She fell and broke her hip last summer and I started driving up every weekend to make sure the housekeeper was taking care of her. Karl's brother Bubba was working like crazy, plus he was dating three girls plus whatever he could pick up on the side. He was out every night to some bar. He kept the ranch running, I'll give him that. Maybe when you're twenty-five you can do it, or maybe a ranch is too much responsibility when you're twenty-five. Anyway, Karl's subdivision in Laramie was a big success—professors from the university and new people all needed houses and it worked just the way it was supposed to.

I loved Alice and nobody in the world loved Toby more. Toby would climb up on Gram's bed and bring a magazine and she would "read" to Gram and they would discuss it. And they played this game of solitaire with no rules, but Toby learned the suits and how to count. And Gram would put lipstick and powder on her and fix her hair in a fancy do and Toby would rub lotion on Gram's hands.

Then Alice died in November and Karl just fell apart. I thought he didn't care about her all these years because he ignored her and I tried to make up for that by visiting and taking Toby and having Alice stay with us before she fell. All his buried emotions came out after she died. He wanted me to quit working—it looked like he wasn't a success if his wife had to work. I decorated the house. Well, when I finally bought furniture it was top-of-the-line Sears and good quality carpeting, but "decorating" is maybe too definite a word. I asked friends for suggestions. The house looks homey with paintings and photographs and Toby's art and dried flowers and my friends know I need them, because they saw what I did on my own: nothing. Just Southwestern designs—some terra cotta pottery, bright wool wall hangings to brighten the gray winters. It looks okay to me. Anyway, I bought better clothes, but Karl didn't understand that I wanted to stop working and I couldn't—I'd lose myself if I did. I don't like the person I am without it. If I was going to quit, I could have done it sooner. If I can't get outdoors, I get crazy after a while.

Anyway, he's starting to spend time on the phone and I think he's got a new project, something in Jackson Hole. I hope he pulls out of this depression.

In the meantime Toby is wonderful, with big dark eyes and straight blond hair. She's reading a little and her day care is Montessori and she's a happy little person, especially when she gets her way.

Have a good New Year.

—Jess

**Merry Christmas and Happy New Year - 1972**

Now I know how it felt when the Roman Empire collapsed. I may end up taking school pictures yet.

Love—Kip

Christmas 1973

It feels funny, Kip, sending a bad photo to a good photographer, but this is Toby's school picture and I wanted you to see how beautiful she is. Karl's project in Jackson Hole is bogged down, but I've gone up another two grades, so the money is good and there's more work. At least it's an interesting project, related to coal mining, and should go on for years. I don't know if this will find you in London, but I'm sending it with much love.

—Jess

**Merry Christmas and Happy New Year - 1973**

Switzerland was great, learned all the different wines. Hiked with climbers up the Matterhorn. Had to buy them bright-colored jackets before we left so they'd show up.

Love—Kip

Christmas 1974

Kip—

Glad to hear you're happy in London. Tell Megan she's getting a wonderful guy. No changes here in God's Country, except Karl's project proceeds very slowly and Toby gets prettier.

—Jess

**Merry Christmas and Happy New Year-1974**

Christmas in Nepal is almost as exotic as L.A. Megan sent Toby a present, which will probably arrive next summer.

She misses teaching and kids, but is recovering.

Love—Kip

Christmas 1975

Dear Kip, this isn't my Xerox-a-bunch-of-copies Christmas letter. I have an appointment for me and my lawyer with Karl and his lawyer. It only takes twenty-one days to get divorced in Wyoming, if you're a resident, but it's taking longer than that to work out the settlement and I'm going nuts. Karl put the subdivision in Laramie in my name for taxes (some hotshot advisors), and now he's trying to get it back, of course. I was going to give it and anything else he wanted just to get out of this, but my attorney, bless her heart, was smarter than I was. Karl is trying to hurt me with money. It means so much to him, he thinks it should mean a lot to me. Plus in a divorce, everything gets reduced to money because the courts can deal with that. Not holding my hand when I was in labor or Christmas dinner at the ranch or Bubba's wedding or struggling together—just dollars. But I'm holding out for a big settlement, which I can put away for Toby. When she's ready for college, it'll mean she has options she wouldn't have otherwise. It's all ugly and exhausting and I'll be glad when it's over.

I'm trying not to be bitter or angry but it's just too hard to admit I made so many mistakes. And in the meantime, I started seeing a man, another mistake I won't go into. Karl kept spending more and more time in Jackson. He lost his shirt on the condo—I don't know how because people pay so much for real estate there. But eventually he moved into one of the units, already occupied by a rich man's daughter who was crazy for skiing. Daddy thought she'd be safer in Jax than Los Angeles. Jax is just Beverly Hills with mountains.

My folks have been wonderful. They'll keep Toby when we go to court and then Mom is coming here for a couple of weeks. Thank God I have friends to talk to when I get crazy. And I have work that absorbs me.

I haven't even asked how you're doing. I scan photo credits and read the sideways print next to photographs, looking for your name. I can't resist six-point type—I also read survivors of airplane disasters and lists of bills approved by the city council and representatives to state leadership camps.

Stay with me if you're out this way. That didn't come out right. I must admit that I talk to you in my head. You know I'm a straightforward person, no imagination. But I have all these unapproved and censored and X-rated and awful, wicked, evil things in my head. And I tell them to you in my mind.

I know it's not the real you—we just barely stay in touch and if we got together it probably would be really awkward. But as long as you are somewhere in the world, I have you, to keep like a good luck charm in the bottom of my jewelry box. I shouldn't say all this, but I want you to know you're important to me—that it's important you're somewhere, taking pictures.

Love—Jess

# 11

*"Your call last week* felt like Christmas lasted until January." Jess stood at the kitchen counter and looked at the new 1976 calendar next to the fridge. She could see into the family room where Toby watched "The Electric Company" on TV. Barbie dolls and clothes lay scattered all over the floor. "You always sent a Christmas card, so at least I knew you were alive."

"Sometimes it was the only card I sent," Kip answered.

"Then I would send you pages and pages of news of everything that happened in the last year."

"I loved those letters."

"Where are you now?"

"Denver airport. Waiting for my flight back to Washington. I'll collect Megan, then I'm going to be photo editor of the *Post* beginning the first of the month."

"That sounds great! You always liked it out here. Maybe there's a backpacking trail the tourists haven't destroyed."

"That was a thought I had."

"What does Megan think?"

"She thinks there are schools and churches and people who need a music teacher in Denver. She's already talking to Regis College and the city school district, whatever it's called. I hope she can breathe—that was another thought. Once people with asthma came to Denver to recover. They still have the best asthma specialists here."

"Is hers bad?"

"Bad," he said.

"When *Life* died, I was afraid for you. Was free-lancing hard?"

"Hard enough. I got a healthy severance pay. Everybody was fired. Some of us were hired back on contract to the corporation."

Kip shifted in the crowded alcove, wishing it was quieter. People walking at a purposeful pace streamed past him. He wondered if his flight was late. The sealed windows of the terminal couldn't quite block the smell of airplane fuel exhaust.

"Really, you must have had it rough," she insisted.

"All the photographers on staff, everybody was shocked. We didn't really believe it would happen, then they hit us, like a two-by-four upside your head."

"Which was when you went to Europe." Jess was trying to sort out what she remembered.

"I played around for a while, living in L.A., it was easy. Then I took the *Geographic* assignment and I was out of the country. And met Megan."

"Working in London."

"She thought I was a cowboy because of my American accent and boots." Kip could hear the television music behind Jess's voice. "I worried about you when you were going through the divorce. There was stuff in your letters that I ignored at the time, but later, I could read between the lines."

Jess's voice became deceptively light, disguised. "Those letters were funny. When will we see you both?"

"We'll be coming through Cheyenne next summer," Kip said, watching the airport activity. "There's a photo workshop, sort of a deductible vacation for teachers, in Montana in July. Megan and I will drive up and I'll show her some of Wyoming and we'll camp."

"Stop here so I can meet her and you can see Toby. That would be great!"

"They're calling my flight."

"Take care of yourself!" She was breathless to say one more thing.

"I quit smoking and I jog every day," he said.

"I hike and this winter I'm cross-country skiing."

"We'll be healthy old geezers," he said. "Kiss Toby for me."

Kip sat in his window seat, the drone of the engines in his head, watching the airplane's shadow on the tan patchwork of yellow fields below. He was still wired from interviews. How could he have known, that night in London when he met Megan, that he'd be back in the West?

It had started at one of the inevitable parties young Americans were invited to, in a trendy row house in Chelsea with girls in miniskirts, mink eyelashes, and no-color lips who offered too much to drink, sometimes drugs, and usually sex.

They were taking a break on the front stoop. He waited for a public schools accent, some clever line, but she simply stood there, staring down the street of brick-front houses. He wondered if she was impressed with his shoulder-length hair, his full-sleeved paisley shirt, his velvet bell-bottom trousers.

"Nice night," Kip said.

The girl started, then nodded. He waited for a reply, but she did not speak.

"Noisy party," he said. And again she nodded, but said nothing.

Perhaps she wanted him to leave. He had just about decided he'd had enough of this party but would try once more. "Good music."

"Would you like to take me home?" she asked. Her voice was silver, exquisitely British.

Kip was surprised. "Sure. Do you have a coat?"

"Could we have a cup of tea first? I don't like liquor. Megan Glynn," she said and offered her hand.

From that night she collected Kip in her silences. She was a student from Hyderabad. Her mother was Indian and a sculptor, her father a British engineer. She was in her third year at university and she was always cold. She missed the heat of home and the warmth of family. She studied music and played several instruments, planned to teach.

Kip savored the courtship dance. He moved toward her, she retreated. He waited, she came forward. It seemed to go very slowly, and Kip knew he'd be sent on another assignment. He didn't want her to forget him. He said:"You should have visited London in the Victorian days when you could have worn enough clothes to stay warm. These styles are wonderful to look at, but tights don't keep you very warm."

He ordered long johns from Sears, and she wore them at home and to sleep in. Mostly, she wore ubiquitous jeans and Carnaby Street sweaters, shrunk to fit. He ordered a sheepskin jacket for her, from a place in Taos, which made her seem very stylish. She drank gallons of tea to warm herself and occasionally would try cognac.

He went to the Middle East, but the assignment was aborted when fighting broke out in Lebanon. He came back to London angry at his editors, disgusted with politics, and ready to quit.

"You can't do that," Megan said.

"Oh yes I can." Kip walked beside her to a restaurant in her student neighborhood. His shoulders were stiff with repressed anger.

"No. You need to take photographs. You'd take them even if you weren't paid."

"Fat chance."

"I would make music even if I weren't paid."

"That's different. You're an artist. I'm a journalist. I do this for a living."

"You can't help seeing the way you do, and I think you should print some of those photographs they killed."

"Why bother?"

"To validate what you do."

Kip looked at her. They kept walking, but he considered what she said.

"I've had assignments killed before," he said on the way to the restaurant, which had a curry that Megan said was mild but that took the top of Kip's head off. "It's no big deal."

"If it's no big deal, why do you look ready to kill?"

"I'm okay. Leave me alone."

"Just this once, try it."

"Will you quit!" He didn't like her needling and his voice rose in spite of himself.

"No. You stubborn, bullheaded idiot."

Kip turned on his heel and marched the other way. He was ready to break her in half on a public street. He hadn't known she could be so nasty.

He looked back and she was calmly walking away, to the restaurant, he presumed. He felt sheepish. He had been on the edge of an explosion since he was called back from the assignment.

He ran to catch up with her.

"I'll do it, but I don't think it makes any difference," he said.

He got contact sheets, marked his choices, and paid to have the photos printed—something he hadn't done in years. And he was surprised that Megan was right. He needed to do it. His work had intrinsic worth, no matter what the editors said. He'd save them for a gallery show.

When he asked her how she knew what was good for him, she shrugged and smiled.

He couldn't quite articulate what he felt. Megan cared about what was good for him. She was a buffer against all that the world and editors could do to him.

Kip had never known a woman so exotic, so contained, so silent. She never chattered or seemed to expect him to talk. She carried on intelligent conversation, answered when he spoke, asked for what she wanted. She wasn't secretive but she made no extraneous talk. He opened himself to her and told her his stories—at first to impress her, then to reveal himself.

He had never felt comfortable talking about his dreams and fantasies. She accepted them, demanded honesty, and he gave it. He found balm in her silence. And she told him her stories, in a voice like a flute. Her calm absorbed him and he felt solace for all the griefs of his life.

He thought he had been happy enough before he met her, and he did enjoy the long *National Geographic* assignments which kept him traveling for months. Now he did not want to leave his London base to travel with writers to Nepal or Bulgaria. He asked her to move in, to be there when he returned, but she insisted she keep her own place. Her parents wouldn't understand, she said, and she wouldn't compromise the truth with them.

He saw a handsome, delicate woman with dark hair and eyes and olive skin. He had thought she might be Italian or Spanish. Her skin took the light strangely. She let him photograph her, was indifferent. And the prints never looked right. It was as though she absorbed light, as well as sound, and he misjudged the exposure or the angle of the light. He destroyed most of his prints of her. When she finally had a portrait made for her parents at graduation, it looked to Kip like another woman.

"You don't talk much," Kip said, early on. They were eating pasta in an English Italian restaurant, which never seemed quite right to Kip, who was used to brittle bread sticks, shakers of Parmesan, and Frank Sinatra on the stereo.

"I don't mean to be unfriendly," she said. "Usually, I'm just thinking."

"What do you think about?"

"Music."

"Do you think of how it's made or how you want to play it or how it got written?"

"I think *it*. I hear music in my head. All musicians do."

Kip was jealous that she had her own preoccupations and wasn't thinking of him. Then he remembered how Jess had reacted when he'd told her he was constantly taking pictures in his head.

He thought of Jess—the last woman he had gotten this close to. It hadn't happened in New York, not really, although he had been intimate with several women there. Nor in California. There was a woman at the Ansel Adams Institute, where he tried fine art photography after *Life* died, but she was married and disappeared back into her own life. Jess was a warm memory of a time of freedom and no responsibility.

The better Kip knew Megan, the more he loved her. He found much to admire, but he was most intrigued with the intense sensuality beneath her cool exterior. She never did more that take his arm in public. She never clung to him or demanded tribute. She was almost icily independent. But alone, in his bed, the mask fell away. She told him she loved him, but could not tell him why any more than he could tell her how at home he felt in her silences.

Their relationship grew until Kip, even accustomed as he was to travel, could scarcely bear to leave London. Then he knew he had to commit himself to Megan or lose her. After much personal agonizing, he took her to a posh restaurant and afterward, in her living room over restorative tea, which she poured with the grace of a duchess, he proposed. He was stunned when she refused.

"Don't you love me?" he asked.

"More than anything."

"Then why not?"

"If I married you, I would be alone too much. I would sink into music and make myself busy so I wouldn't miss you. I would constantly have to adapt from being alone to having you here. I would be crazy." Her upper class diction always sounded clear and cool, and tonight it chilled Kip.

"I love you." He wished for eloquence. "I want to be with you. This is my profession."

"I can't marry you." Tears rolled down her face, but her voice was silver, steady and without vibrato. "I love you too much to say good-bye. Each time you left, I would die and a ghost would walk around in my skin, living, studying, practicing."

"I can't—"

"Perhaps we can think of a way to be together. Or a way to part."

And it stayed like that. Megan graduated, and her parents flew from Hyderabad for a week, and he met them—solid people who made him feel at home. He didn't want to think about losing her, and he didn't want to think about working differently.

*Life* had been the pinnacle for a photographer. He remembered the day he had gotten the phone call after Christmas in 1972 telling him that it would cease publishing. He was painting the wood trim around the ceiling of the bedroom in his Laurel Canyon house. He had heard whispers but discounted them. The news was like an earthquake.

He stopped painting three-fourths of the way across the top and never finished it in all the time he lived there. Every time he went to bed, he looked up and saw it unfinished. Later, he told people he had taken his severance pay and done drugs for a year in Laurel Canyon, and people believed him. He did some drugs, but his cure for depression was mountains. A friend took him fishing up in the Cascades and that became his drug. He went to Carmel for the institute and looked at other people's beautiful photographs of seashores and mountains and people dressed and nude. He got raves from the staff for his work but found it too precious and a little dull. He was a journalist.

He left early. He tried saltwater fly fishing and took two weeks to get back to L.A., working his way down the coast.

When Kip got a call from the assistant photo editor at the *Geographic* he took the assignment because he wanted to work. Work was the best cure he could think of for depression. The first assignment kept him for three months in Istanbul, and he got used to the food and enjoyed the mountains and the country people. He got high a lot, because it was so easy to get dope there, but it wasn't the blot-out drugs he'd done in L.A.

He found a place in London and checked with the Washington office each time he returned. Had his bed-sitter apartment been burglarized? If not, he would eat heavy English food and resuscitate his social life. By the time he met Megan, in the summer of seventy-four, he'd more or less gotten used to not being a *Life* photographer. The *Geographic* assignments were fine.

Then he had to think of a way to be with Megan and that meant giving up this newly forged routine, this spurious security, disregarding the reputation he'd built, ignoring that fact that an important magazine published his work.

Starting again.

And then Megan got sick.

First it was a cough, then bronchitis, and after that went on long enough, the diagnosis was asthma. She was teaching in a suburban school district, two elementary schools and a middle school—band and choral singing, or whatever they called it here. Kip wondered how, with her exquisite sensibilities and perfect pitch, could she listen to children sing and play off key all day.

She loved teaching and was very effective. She took on a Lutheran choir and accompanied friends at recitals.

She did stay busy, as she had promised him she would when he was gone, until one day she simply couldn't get out of bed.

When he got home from Novosibirsk she was out of the hospital but not back at work.

He was shaken to his depths. She had been seriously ill and not only had he not been available to her, he had not even known. The thought of living without her was unbearable. He flew to Washington, set up appointments with newspaper editors and publishers with help from people he knew at *Geographic*, and returned to London.

"You will resent doing this, and you'll hate me," Megan said.

She was ready to go back to work, in classrooms fogged with chalk dust full of sneezing, virus-laden children. She had cleaned her apartment, and it felt cold without the litter of sheet music and newspapers and books that usually covered the end tables and shelves. She wore, he remembered, a dress that was architecturally severe, a hard-finish knit of a regal purple.

"We'll get married at the registry office. Phone your parents. We'll fly them over."

"You can't do this!"

"I already have. I'll even get a haircut."

"I never asked for this. I don't want it."

"You'll never get rid of me. This is one way to stay together. Which is what I want. Don't you want it?"

"You're just upset because I was in hospital."

"Damn right. Are you going to promise you'll never get that sick again?"

"I can't promise, of course."

She had turned around on the piano bench and sat slumped, her legs sprawled out, her hands hanging between her blue denim thighs. The lamp over the sheet music backlit her hair and threw her face into shadow. Kip thought he might weep from love or throw himself on the floor and roll around like a dog and howl —anything that would show her how profoundly he wanted to do this.

"I'm thirty-one," he said. "That age beyond which no one is to be trusted. I need to settle down. Get a mortgage, kids, a station wagon, turn into my father." He grinned at the idea. "I've lived outside the States long enough. I want to go back."

"But you could work for any magazine, live anywhere. Why give up everything to live in the West? You need to be in New York."

"Then I'd still be gone all the time, not as long maybe, but gone. Let me see if this will work. Give it a chance. I'll make a bargain with you: if I hate it, if I really do miss this life, I will tell you. Or if you hate it. We'll leave. You can teach anywhere with your credentials."

She turned back to the keyboard.

Maybe she was right, Kip thought, maybe he'd resent having to do this. Maybe he'd hate it. Or maybe he needed to get out in the mountains and put a dry fly on a line and think like a trout.

He needed clear air and dazzling sunlight and someplace of his own that was not an airport waiting room. He wanted to see rose-brown adobe buildings and coyote fences and deer that wasn't stuffed and hanging on a wall. He wanted to hike until his thighs ached, and fall instantly asleep with wood smoke like incense in his tent. He wanted—perhaps—to leave the cameras at home.

Megan agreed that day, after much more talk. The Glynns flew in for the brief ceremony and celebration. Kip's father flew in from Chevy Chase, and they made a strangely cohesive family. Their friends teased that they got married in such a hurry because Megan must be pregnant. Then they flew to Washington, where they stayed with friends while Kip met with prospective employers.

Megan had one attack while he was in Billings. Friends reassured him in Albuquerque that she was okay. In Fort Worth, he bought her silly souvenirs—coffee mugs with armadillos and cactus-shaped pot holders.

He took a position on the *Denver Post* and phoned Jess. Later he and Megan bought a house in Lakewood, a pleasant suburb, and settled down to a quiet life.

Megan taught a full load in the music department at Denver University and conducted one church choir. Kip was assistant photo editor, then photo editor, and hiker of wilderness trails. Megan joined him for fishing trips. Her asthma attacks were manageable and he was never away from her for more than a day or two at a time.

"I can't shift gears," he said in exasperation, soon after he started.

"What's wrong with the car?" she asked.

"Shift gears in my head." He rubbed the labrador's head, and the dog wriggled in delight.

"What's wrong?"

Megan stopped chopping whatever it was for dinner and put down the chef's knife. She walked over to Kip and slid her thin arms around him. It was silent comfort. A woman who is made of music values silence, the still point of the dance.

"Tell me." She kissed the bony ridge of his collarbone, since it was handiest.

"I thought the daily deadline would be the hard part, but I just slipped into that rhythm. But the paper! The newsprint won't take detail. The fine, artistic effects you can get on slick paper are impossible on that paper. And I'm used to exercising a certain esthetic judgment. That's what they hired me for."

Megan fetched a can of beer, popped it open, and handed it to him. Then she resumed chopping. She made vaguely Indian dishes from time to time and while they tasted okay, curry wasn't Kip's favorite seasoning.

"So eventually your head will shift and you can look at these photographs as something different." Megan nibbled celery. "You can exercise your esthetic judgment on newsprint. Or on your own work. That was devilishly clever of you, to negotiate for assignment time without relinquishing leave time."

"I don't know if I'll get that many calls, but I want to keep my hand in. What's that on the radio?"

"Bartok."

"I thought his stuff sounded like fists on the keyboard. I'm worried. This is starting to sound like music."

"Philistine!"

Kip put his hands around her waist. He could feel the bony knobs of her hipbones. She was wheezing a little.

After a year, when Megan didn't get pregnant, they began fertility testing. Kip didn't care so much, but he knew she wanted children. He was afraid she wasn't healthy enough to carry a child to term.

He was waiting when she came back from the doctor. She dropped her purse on the kitchen counter and hung up her coat. She looked diminished, as though she had shrunk inside her clothes. Huge gray circles surrounded her eyes.

"What did the doctor say?" Kip couldn't keep the edge out of his voice. He went over to her.

"Congenital anomalies," Megan said. She looked drained.

"Which means?"

"No babies." Tears ran down her face, and she reached for the tissue box. Kip tried to put his arms around her. She shrugged him off, and he felt betrayed. She stayed tense as she continued: "The doctor says he never says 'never,' but the chances of my carrying a baby to term were remote. Was that the word? Anyway, it isn't you."

"I don't care."

"Care what?"

"I love you. I don't care if we have kids."

"I thought you wanted them! Why have we been going through all this medical nonsense?"

"Because you wanted it. I mean, I like kids and always thought we'd have kids, but if it doesn't happen, that's okay. I hate to think of the strain on you—with asthma."

He could see her stiffen.

"God gave you a beautiful face, a lovely body, and crummy lungs. All that IQ, all that talent and sensitivity and these anomalies. Nobody asks us, 'Which would you rather be? Lucky or smart? Pretty or healthy?' Maybe somebody does, but by the time we get born we forget. So we're stuck with what we've got. Get mad, scream, pound the piano, whatever it takes—but it's okay with me. As you are, however that is. Just remember that."

She turned away from him and went upstairs. Her

reserve protected her against minor and daily assaults but shut him out when the blow was as heavy as this. He wanted to comfort her. He knew he didn't feel it as she did, couldn't. All he could do was stand with her and console her if she could let him.

He opened a Coors and turned on the John Chancellor news. Later, he made a sandwich and fell asleep watching an old movie. Then, in the night, he woke up stiff-necked on the couch. He heard her playing through the closed door. He tiptoed into the family room. She paused, then resumed playing.

He walked over and found space on the piano bench. It was Chopin—now crystalline runs, now rattling chords, a pounding march. The music reached where words couldn't go. When she finished the piece, she raised her hands gracefully from the keys.

"I can't accept it," she said. This was as much as her reserve would allow her to say. Her voice shook, and she stopped.

He said nothing. The music still rang in his ears.

Then she put her arms around him and he held her as she wept. He hated it when she cried, but if she didn't, she would die. It frightened him that she felt so much pain. When the repressed emotions boiled up from beneath that polished facade at last, they shook her whole body. She keened like a coyote. His shirt was wet with her tears. Her fingernails dug into his back. When she paused to gasp, he picked her up and held her like a child, hoping he was brave enough to last out the storm.

# 12

*Kip enjoyed Denver*, his first attempt to put down roots. They didn't have much money, but Megan flourished, despite her disappointment over not being able to have children. She grew healthy, even gained weight. She still looked delicate, but not ill. Her work at the university was demanding, and she often complained about tokenism and the old boys' club atmosphere, but she returned to the fray each semester.

One day soon after they bought the house in Lakewood, Kip came home to find Megan on a stepladder with a new staple gun in her hand. She had changed into jeans and one of his old shirts.

"What are you doing?"

"Wiring the house."

"Don't we have electricity?"

"This is for speakers."

She climbed down, moved the ladder, and continued stapling wire around the baseboards and up the stairs.

"I hope nothing happens to either of us, because we owe a lot of money to A B & K Service Inc.," she said.

"We do?" Kip sat in the living room in a shabby chair, and the dog insinuated his head under Kip's hand. Kip scratched around Jasper's ears and watched Megan, admiring the line of her thigh, the delicacy of her ankle, the light coming from upstairs making her hair gleam. She was awkward but effective with the staple gun, which looked too heavy for her thin wrists and fine hands. She stopped to pull out a misplaced staple.

"I bought a lot of expensive equipment. I decided I wanted to go ahead."

"Yeah, we talked, but I thought you'd have it installed."

"I'm perfectly capable of doing this. Besides, I know what I want."

They went out for pizza that night when she finally took a break. For the next week, she hammered and installed shelves and hardware and when she was finished, the whole house was wired. She could switch music wherever she wanted it, from the decks in the music room. The room off the kitchen of the split-level was usually a family room, but since it was the only room that comfortably held the grand piano and all the books and sheet music, plus a cello and flute and recorders and music stands, it was the music room.

Megan usually got home before he did; although the *Post* was a morning paper he worked a modified day-schedule, arriving home around seven in the evening. He knew she was home when he heard music murmuring somewhere in the house.

If they didn't start ripping their clothes off too quickly, Megan would playfully program fucking music—old Sinatra or fifties jazz—into the bedroom. She played rock 'n' roll when she cleaned house but listened to the radio when they cooked and ate dinner. She became a connoisseur of country-western and Kip laughed till tears ran when she sang the lugubrious lyrics in her crisp Brit accent.

Megan practiced the piano daily, although she did not play in public any more. Mostly he heard classical music coming from the music room, blending in with the rest of the environment—the smell of dinner, or the laundry detergent when the drier ran, or the dust in the carpets. It was part of the fabric of his life, along with the ticking of the dog's claws on the kitchen floor. First, it was in his ears, then in his head.

He never disliked classical music, but he didn't have Megan's encompassing interest in it. Sometimes he listened to hard rock, heavy metal—Led Zeppelin, Van Halen, even Alice Cooper—anything to get away from the discipline of classical music. He liked folk singers who accompanied themselves and Patsy Cline, John Hartford bluegrass banjo pickers, lounge crooners, jazzy ladies like Sarah and Lena and Ella. He liked Jerry Lee Lewis pounding on the piano, Little Richard's falsetto squeal and Big Maybelle and John Lee Hooker—although some of it was tough to find.

He liked Art Tatum and Charlie Parker and Dave Brubeck and especially Chet Baker and new jazz musicians coming along faster than he could remember names. Mostly he didn't like in-between music—watery symphony orchestras playing Beatles. The Boston Pops was a fat dowager trying to boogie. Muzak didn't register, except as an irritation.

All sound was music to Megan. She liked their lab because Jasper almost never barked. When he did it was true communication, not just another noise. She insulated herself with sound, kept the world away while she healed each day's strains and demands.

Kip insisted they not take a portable radio or cassette player with them into the mountains. He said moving water was the purest music. She granted this but seemed strained without the tranquilizing effect of habitual music—a junkie whose supply is cut off. After a half dozen trips to fishing streams, where she learned to imitate what he did but did not understand it, she turned off the car radio as soon as they pulled out of the driveway. He fished, they hiked, she wrote letters to Hyderabad.

She went to one of the asthma specialists who was on staff at National Jewish Hospital. She consistently took her breathing treatments and meds and walked for exercise. Sometimes they made love with Kip in strange positions, so she could sit up. She would ask if he felt like "doing yoga" that night. But still, when the pollen was heavy in the spring and during hay fever season, he noticed that she used the inhaler oftener. If the stress at school got out of hand, it showed up in wheezing. Every time she went into the hospital he thought she would die. She would struggle, cough, and still not get enough oxygen until her dark skin looked blue-gray.

They would start antibiotics and prednisone, a steroid which immediately pulled her out of the attack. But no one could take megadoses of that drug for long. Then she would apologize and he would take her out of town for a weekend and she would settle down. He noticed she almost inevitably had an attack after the spring term was over. One summer she did not teach and she was better the next fall.

He resented being whipsawed—from afraid she would die to relief that she would live—sometimes in a few hours. He knew she couldn't help it. Sometimes he knew when she was sickening before she did and tried to slow her down. But there were so many things to do and so many students and so much music.

Sometimes he wondered how he had "fallen" from *Life* to photo editor at a large city daily. Perhaps not a fall, but definitely a lateral shift. His job was to make sure that photos got taken and printed on the sports pages. He missed exercising his own creativity and was glad he could take a few assignments.

He still went back to work at the M.U. photo workshop in the fall. After several visits, he returned annually as part of the faculty. He kept in touch with Edom, who aged slowly and nurtured new photographers.

He thought of other photographers who had *Vogue* assignments and gallery shows in New York. He thought of *People* magazine starting up. He got calls from galleries in Scottsdale and Santa Fe, and sometimes mounted a show—western landscapes, critter pictures, and occasional portraits. In the late seventies, he began workshops in which he guided participants into wilderness areas to shoot photographs, not animals.

Kip often missed the old life and wondered if this had been the right decision. He had his dog and friends and fishing. He and Megan bought a small cabin near Fairplay where they could go for weekends, but he planned more elaborate trips into Montana or New Mexico when he had the time to backpack into wilderness.

He got calls from Washington and New York and took photo assignments if he could. He helped visiting colleagues and kept his contacts alive. If he had stuck pins in a map for every friend, contact, or colleague, the United States would have been studded throughout, more heavily on both coasts. A friend from Bogota once told him a proverb: Friends are better than money. He hadn't planned to live by it, but that was how things worked out.

Megan asked from time to time if he was sorry. Each time he thought, then said, no. After a while he said no even when he didn't know if he still meant it.

One day early in the spring seventy-seven semester, a little more than three years after they had moved to Denver, Megan came in, dropped her briefcase, and rushed to the kitchen where Kip was inventing stir-fried bean tortillas. She threw her arms around him from behind and said, "The most wonderful thing happened today!"

"Tell me," he said. He put down his spatula and turned to hug her. The trees in the backyard stood bare, and the iron sky said spring would never come. Jasper was sleeping under the piano, looking like a huge furry stuffed toy. The Bee Gees throbbed from the stereo.

"This student showed up for chorus tryouts. I have never seen him in any music classes. An older student, in a program for retraining. He's on disability from a construction job."

"You know all this already?"

"I talked to him after the audition. I could *not* believe his voice. He didn't have any music for the accompanist, so I asked him to just sing as he usually did. So he sang a hymn a capella. Said the only singing he did was at church. I asked him to sing another song and he asked if I wanted his 'opera voice,' and I said sure, so it was almost like Gomer Pyle—he went from this normal, soft spoken voice with Hispanic nasals into, into—Caruso."

Kip felt her forehead with the back of his hand to show that he thought she was loco. Megan laughed and kissed him. She took off her suit jacket and tied on an apron.

"I had him sing different songs—he can sing pops, Spanish love ballads, church hymns—each in a different voice. He can't read music! He can't even read music!"

"A shortcoming you will promptly cure."

"Of course. It's like finding a buried treasure. First I'll see if he really wants to learn to sing well, give him a couple of solos and maybe next semester, try some private lessons."

Megan's interest in Aquilino Valdez grew. He was an eager student. Kip was jealous that this kid could inspire enthusiasm from Megan that he couldn't, or didn't any more. But it was a different order of interest. Aquilino was stocky, his neck short and his inky hair straight, cut to cover his ears. He wore a distinctive straw Stetson all year round. He smiled easily and joked with Megan. He could sing like an angel but refused to give up his motorcycle or his barrio friends and their weekend parties.

Kip wondered if Megan and Aquilino were sleeping together, then felt guilty for thinking it. Kip considered his sex life more than satisfactory, except when Megan was ill.

Megan and Aquilino had a master-student element of formality in their relationship. Aquilino respected Megan and her expertise. She adored his voice. Kip didn't want his discontent to spoil Megan's pleasure—the ambiguous delight of finding a student who will surpass the teacher, finding a once-in-a-lifetime voice she lovingly polished and displayed. He only wished she could direct this creative urge to composing.

He tried to get used to the situation and convinced himself that it was good for all of them. One evening as Megan played and Aquilino sang in the music room, he assembled a pot of chili in the kitchen, with the dog underfoot, terribly interested in the hamburger. Kip looked in to see Megan lift her hand lovingly to Aquilino's face. The young man was looking at the music on the piano and couldn't see her expression. Kip could scarcely breathe—it was a mother's look. She stroked Aquilino's face as a mother would a child—for affection, for encouragement, for reward. To let him know he was valued and loved. Kip turned away, shaken.

Aquilino, with Megan's coaching, started to enter competitions. He sang at a glitzy saloon in a hotel on weekends. He wanted to drop out of D.U. and just sing, but Megan persuaded him to stay, found tutors, kept him in his retraining program, which meant money for school. Aquilino trusted Megan. He also depended on her. He also confessed to her—the women, which she tried to be broad-minded about, and dope, which she had no patience for. Eventually, he would have to leave the security of Denver if he wanted a singing career. Megan had no doubt that he could succeed if he decided to do it.

Kip couldn't deny her something that brought so much joy. She had given up everything to follow him to the States. "Whither thou goest" to the tenth power. Why had he thought it would work? Why hadn't he known he would feel a ripple of guilt forever? He knew that Megan missed London and her friends there, but mostly she missed Hyderabad.

They saved for trips and in between their trips, the Glynns visited Colorado. James Glynn took to trout fishing immediately, and Megan and her mother chattered constantly about all the things that had happened that hadn't gone into the long, long letters.

Kip had always been taken by Megan's silences, and she was still a contained, quiet woman—until her mother arrived. Then she became the animated girl she must have been before she left home.

He knew what it cost him to choose this life when he compared it to what his other colleagues were doing. When the Glynns visited, he got a glimpse of what it cost Megan to leave all she knew, marry him, and live in Denver.

Their compromises were too heavy a burden for love to carry. Like a caryatid, the stone maiden holding up the temple roof, love faltered, unequal to that weight. Over the years they built other supports of mutual affection, shared experiences, sexual comfort. So the marriage survived—a little shaky, but standing.

In a couple of years Aquilino would leave Denver. In the meantime, he attracted attention from agents and scouts. Megan recommended caution. Aquilino wanted to make money.

Kip noted the asthma attacks were coming more often. He wondered how much her battered lungs could take, how long her immune system could fight, how hard her heart could beat.

Since Megan was happy, Kip smothered the unsettled feeling he got every time she said she was tired, every time they decided not to go to the movies, not to meet friends, not to make love. She was working very hard. She always worked as hard as her health allowed. She had ended up in the hospital once when she took on a second choir. She pretty much knew her limits but always wanted to do more. Kip knew her limits even better than she did because her wishes didn't obscure what he saw.

If he hadn't loved her, he still would have cared for

her. She was an intensely focused woman who accomplished good things—with her classes, with her choir, with her colleagues. Her integrity demanded that people give her their best. Hadn't she enchanted him so that he had given his best self? So, just because she was worthy, he would have taken care of her. But he still loved her, with the edges smoothed down by years of habit, and reconciliations, sex and food and fun and friends. Years of trips to Fairplay where the creek's music, the clear air, and the trees' whispers healed them both. Years of meals together, years of nights in the same bed, always. Years of accommodating each other.

When he saw the circles under her eyes darken, he became afraid. The first shiver of apprehension started up his back. Then she began coughing. He checked the weather, the air-quality level, the pollen count. If it was relatively clear, another shiver began, the cellos behind the violins. Then when she turned on the vaporizer and sucked her spray more often, the bass drum began a hollow throb.

He tried to slow her down, suggested that he do the chores, tried to lure her to a concert to rest for a few hours. The wheezing worsened, and tension trembled from the woodwinds. If she didn't quit, her asthma quit for her and she went to bed. Then Kip's anxiety was complete—brass and tympani, winds and strings going full blast, a Mahler finale of layers and layers of tension until his gut was solid ice.

Megan looked like a ghost then. Gray-faced, colorless lips, pale eyelids. He hated to go to work, but she had an emergency alarm that would fetch an ambulance.

He blamed himself that she was sick. Denver wasn't a forgiving place to live. Thermal inversions trapped brown pollution for weeks in the mountain bowl that held the city. If he hadn't come here, if he hadn't insisted they get married, if she hadn't committed herself to him. If, if, if.

Then he would stop, pull himself together and take over until she recovered. A day or two in the hospital, until the infection was under control.

Once home, he would bring trays up to her bed and sleep in the guest bedroom. He kept the dog away. He screened her calls. She improved until one day he couldn't hold her back any longer and she returned to classes, already under stress from backed-up classwork.

But if it made her happy to coach Aquilino and fuss over him then Kip would make it possible for her to do it, and he would ignore his unsettled feeling.

Aquilino would come over at night and work his way through a new aria or song. Megan's patience for him never wore thin. Kip scheduled his daily runs during the lessons. He would lace up his running shoes and pound the quiet suburban streets, and after a mile or so the runner's rhythm kicked in.

During these long, mind-loosening runs Jess came back to him. Jess was as solid as the earth—healthy and reliable.

He remembered each fiber of the worn rug in her living room in Casper. It was gray to the backing, then pale. Each wool strand was stiff. He remembered the dust smell, like a vacuum cleaner. He remembered especially how it felt under his elbows and knees. He could feel the rug, but not the rug burn. Not till later, afterward.

He remembered the huffs of Jess's breath—heaving, gasping, damp over his shoulder. He knew the reach of her arms down his back an inch short of his tailbone. He knew to the exact degree the angle of flexibility of her legs, the length of her femur, her cushioned thigh flesh.

He knew the rhythm of involuntary muscle spasms as her body took over and pulsed with his. He respected her body's strength—arched and straining and shuddering.

He remembered the taste of her and her smell in his skin and the sticky softness of her mouth, relaxed and swollen when they stopped.

Then he would find himself circling back to the house, memories so vivid and intense that he hadn't noticed where he had run. He never summoned the memories; they rose up and found him. Sometimes he remembered exactly what they had eaten at a particular meal: heavy beef stew laced with oregano, thickened gravy, big chunks of carrot and potato, wheat bread, butter. Those meals that she cooked with such care.

He remembered the many-times-washed softness of Jess's long johns. They had shrunk until the cotton-wool knit molded itself to her body, the last barrier when clothes came off. Then warm skin replaced the softness of fabric. Jess's skin was always warm and soft. She wore no perfume, and the only scents were a trace of laundry detergent from her clothes or herbs from her shampoo.

He would home in to Casper, drive on automatic to their street, stagger into the apartment. There he fed on her presence, pulled affection through the skin, restored himself with her solid, healthy body, her simple meals, her laundered linen, her love.

His public saintliness admitted these private lapses. The memories were so clean that he forgave himself. He seemed to have no control over them, anyway. And in some way they were a relief valve so that he could bear Megan's interest in Aquilino.

When he got back to the house, Aquilino would be

gone and Megan would be wan with fatigue, so they would eat and she would go to bed. She often fell asleep as soon as she pulled the blanket up. Kip would be half-wired from running and half-wishing for sex but would murmur good night and kiss her forehead.

Each had been unfaithful, but it wasn't a matter of adultery, which has its own folklore and implications. For Kip, it was something dark he couldn't name, something he couldn't talk to Megan about.

She continued to push herself, coaching Aquilino. Gradually, over several years, the young man became a fixture at their dinner table, often cooking Mexican specialties after the session in the music room. He rode through their quiet suburb on a noisy Harley, ruffling the ducks in the little lake in the park. He had nice manners, almost courtly with Megan. He was cheerful, hardworking, and agreeable.

Kip hated him, then hated himself for it. He punished himself with harder runs, to get away from the beautiful, masculine tenor voice. Aquilino sang arias for Megan that were the purest distillation of longing, despair, and love. Kip knew that she responded to music more deeply, on many more levels than he did. If the soaring voice touched him, what did it do to Megan? Did the music reach places where words couldn't go?

Kip tried to mask his childish jealousy.

"Why don't you like Aquilino?" Megan asked one lazy Sunday morning.

"How do you know I don't?" asked Kip, studying the Sunday sports section.

"You hide it well. But you hold back with him. You're a little too polite."

"Politeness is a crime?"

"You aren't answering." She poured herself another

cup of coffee.

"I don't know. He's a nice kid."

"I like him a lot." She stopped and studied Kip. "He's got a voice in a million. I found him. I'm teaching him. It's as close to greatness as I'll come. If he studies, but doesn't overwork his voice, get polyps, if he gets the right seasoning, the right experiences. If the people who make decisions hear him and like him. But it's a chance I must take. Be patient with me. Soon he'll be gone. Isn't there something in *The Prophet* about children like arrows that we shoot into the future? Students, even more than children, are quickly gone."

Kip nodded and mentally beat himself up. He could be patient, but she was having attacks oftener and oftener.

One night when he came in from running and went into the kitchen for water he couldn't help but peek into the music room. Aquilino leaned over the keyboard, studying the music. Megan sat on the bench. Their heads were together and she was resting her hand on his shoulder. Kip felt his gut retract. Megan, who taught other people's children and could have none of her own, had found an outlet for nurturing, different from what she gave Kip, unavailable to him.

He could only watch over her, protect her, and try to keep her from getting ill. When Aquilino finally left for Juilliard, after the performances and farewell parties and gifts and thanks—Megan collapsed. It was exhaustion, plus asthma. She had to cancel summer classes. The infections required stronger drugs.

# 13

*Karl spent so much time* in Jackson that he and Jess were separated long before the divorce, long before she gave up trying to make the marriage work. He was working on his condo-ski lodge in Jackson. At first he came home every weekend, then gradually he spent more time there. She knew she had waited too long when she started dreaming Karl dead.

Jess woke up from a dream in which she wore a black dress and black veil and bent over a casket with Karl's body inside. She was putting something into the coffin, tucking it carefully down the sides next to the satin lining. When she woke she was ashamed and guilty that she wished Karl dead, but after coffee and breakfast she tried to recapture the dream. What had she been pushing into the edges of the coffin? She had several other dreams in which she saw Karl's body in a coffin and then woke up sweating and out of breath, with a queasy feeling that lasted an hour or so.

Karl had been so depressed over his mother's death that Jess had thought he might have had to be hospitalized, but he'd pulled out of the depression and had begun his new project, Antelope Flats. It gradually took more and more of his time, until he opened an office in Jackson to supervise the contractors.

He usually made it home on weekends, but this was the first Friday in a month, and even so he groused about the bad highways and driving in a snowstorm. He had already taken most of his clothes, his hunting gear, and half the camping equipment to Jackson. He had loans and a separate business account at Jackson State Bank. Jess had given up any social life in Cheyenne because Karl was never around. She stayed home with Toby rather than get a sitter to go to a concert or movie alone. Neighborhood cookouts or school potlucks fitted her style, because she could bring Toby along.

That awful January Friday Jess waited till Toby was in bed. On the radio in the kitchen John Denver sang about sunshine. Karl settled in a comfortable chair with papers from his briefcase and a drink. It was his first weekend in Cheyenne since Christmas. Toby had insisted they leave up a Christmas wreath she'd made in Brownies.

"Who is Kathy?" she asked.

Karl looked up and seemed to turn pale. "A woman at Antelope Flats."

"She wants you to pick up some batteries on your way home. I thought this was your home. What's going on?"

Jess felt cold and hollow. She let the long silence grow. Would he try to talk his way out? Would he lie?

"I'm leaving," he finally said.

She heard it but was too shocked for it to register.

"For good? When did you plan to tell me?"

Karl put down the forms he was reading.

"I meant to tell you, but it's just so awkward."

Jess waited, silent. Awkward didn't begin to say it.

"I met this woman," said Karl. "You know how it is, parties and everybody in the lodge in the evenings during the season. I was in Jackson most of the time and hell, it was lonely. When she decided to move to Jackson, I sold her one of the units." He paused and dropped his head. "The one I'm living in is really hers."

Jess drew in a breath. She felt as if she had been stabbed in some vital place and was bleeding, but couldn't feel the pain yet.

"That's what's been keeping you in Jackson, why you're never home?"

He shrugged.

"Do you want a divorce?" she asked, her voice shaky.

He shrugged again. "I guess so."

"You're damned right. I don't put up with this."

"I'll move out tomorrow."

"Is that all you've got to say?"

"What do you want?" He didn't look at her.

"Why? What happened? What went wrong?"

He looked off into the distance. Jess sat on the edge of the couch opposite him. She thought he was finished talking—as much as he ever talked. Then he glanced at her with a look of intense pain. She didn't think eyes could hold that much pain. She didn't think she could face that much.

"This condo deal is going down the tubes." He sighed. "I should have financed it differently. I got overextended. I didn't want to put up the Laramie subdivision, maybe lose both."

Jess hadn't known this.

"You are busy," he continued. "You are always busy. You were busy when we married. You never gave me your full attention. You always had your career, your work in the back of your mind. I couldn't compete with that. I couldn't occupy your mind, keep you interested, twenty-four hours a day. You said you loved me. I know, I know. You *did* love me. You never ignored me. I know you've cried because of the conflict—Toby and me versus the Survey. We won most of the time."

Jess wanted to say it was different—she didn't love working the way she loved him and Toby. But she sensed that if she interrupted, Karl would never say some important things.

"I feel like a jerk—begging for attention, like a little kid, whining. So if I make a bunch of money, that would do it. But you still didn't quit. After a while, I gave up. We had a good life. I was proud of you, doing what only a few women had done before."

He had never told her he was proud. She only remembered the judgmental air, the passive resistance to what she was doing. His way of making it hard to do what she had to do. Making her find day care for Toby even when he was home. She waited, listening.

"When my mother died, I couldn't cope," Karl continued. "It was the death of my childhood. Of a lot of things. All the shit that happened, I never made it right with her. She put up with me raising hell, worse than Bubba, flunking out of school. Yeah, I never graduated. I could never tell you that. You've got a masters. I lost money running the ranch. I mean, we didn't lose any property, but I wasn't a good manager. And my mother never once said anything, she just loved me anyway. So I tried to make it up with you—make money, make the business work. And you loved me anyway, even when I screwed up. I managed to make the Laramie deals work—like magic. I was building in the right place at the right time."

He got up and wandered into the kitchen, made

himself a bourbon and water and came back, still caught in his memories. He didn't put in any ice.

"So when Ma died, I knew I'd lost half of what kept me going—her. You and Toby were the other half. I should have spent more time with her, should have told her how I felt, should have, should have, should have, should have—"

Jess felt tears dam up behind her eyes.

"So this Antelope Flats was going to make up for it. I forced myself to pick up the phone, start in again. Some days I sat at the desk and couldn't pick it up. I kept going to that therapist, but it wasn't getting easier. He said I stopped when I got to the hard parts and I didn't even know what he meant. Finally, I decided I could talk to him and sit in the spare bedroom at my desk forever—I needed to *do* something."

He took a sip of his drink and continued. "It was like starting a snowball with one snowflake. One phone call. Then two. Then four. It's all uphill. Now you pack the snowball with your hands, pick up another layer. Pretty soon it's big enough to roll, roll it every way to make it even. Then suddenly it's bigger than you are and you have to sweat to keep it from rolling downhill, and it takes all you've got."

Jess knew he had been suffering when he was depressed, but he had never told her these things. He never told her anything about himself. Most of what she knew about him came from stories Alice told about when Karl and Bubba were little. Family stories.

"It was starting to roll, the contractors were getting paid, clients were looking. Advertising was pulling in some inquiries. Then the bank called my loan. They can do that. They never do. I mean, nobody could start a business if they called all the loans they could. I cashed in everything, borrowed from Kathy, and made it. And the next month they called the new loan. Somebody wanted Antelope Flats and had enough pull to get it. Kathy came through again. Her father has a lot of money. This was after we started living together."

Jess took deep breaths and forced herself to stay silent. She gripped the edge of the couch cushion, felt the nubby fabric under her nails.

"She's twenty-four. She's ski-crazy. Moved to Jackson for the sports—rafting, climbing—all of it. She doesn't have a career, doesn't care. She think's I'm great. Says her Daddy made and lost three million dollars before he was forty. I couldn't dip into the Laramie situation—you'd find out. Your name is on everything. That's going to complicate things now."

Jess waited. Long minutes passed. Karl drank, finally looked over at her. His pain seared her, but she needed to be strong, not cave in to him, not let pity weaken her.

"And Kathy knew you were having trouble and loved you anyway when you didn't think I would," Jess said.

"Something like that."

"You don't give me much credit."

"It just happened. She was there. I was there. It was nice to be idolized. Kathy is pretty and bright and she thinks I'm great."

Jess couldn't say anything. If she had known this a year ago, she could have been more understanding, more accepting, less pushy about the therapist. Less insistent that he do something, anything, to go back to work.

"I can't go back and do last year differently," said Jess.

"It's already done. Kathy is 'home.' Antelope Flats is home."

"What will you do?"

"Work for her father. Find backing for another condo." He managed a warped grin. "Give ski lessons."

"And all the things we talk about—about the house, about Toby, about Bubba and Alice and the ranch—these never said 'love' to you?"

"I couldn't hear it."

"I guess you couldn't hear how I was hurting, either. I feel bad. I can't feel angry. Not yet. And I will keep Toby."

Only then did he look at her and blink his watery eyes. "No!"

Jess braced herself. In this one last moment of honesty and pain, they broke apart.

"You may get visitation, but you'll never get custody!"

"I'll come and get her."

"Over my dead body. I'll get a restraining order tomorrow."

"You can't take her away!"

"Do you think any judge in Wyoming will let her live with you and your . . . paramour? What kind of environment is that? You hardly know Toby. I take care of her, go to parents night, take her to basketball practice. You don't even know what her shoe size is!"

"But she's my child!" He raised his voice.

"You have no right to her. She has a mother, but you've never been much of a father."

"I haven't? I've supported you, bought you this house. I would have done more if you hadn't been so high and mighty, go-back-to-work, I-have-a-career."

"It's my fault your ego was too fragile?" Jess's throat hurt as she screamed the words. "Who kept everything going while you sat and stared at the walls for two years? If I hadn't been so high and mighty how would we have paid the bills? Where would you have gotten the money to start this project?" Jess was up and pacing in front of the couch.

"You couldn't just do it, you had to throw it up to me."

"I *never* threw it up to you. Until now."

"You never wanted to get it on any more."

"So that gave you the right to get it on with somebody else? When you were depressed you said not to pressure you. Don't you think I missed it? I still felt the same, I just couldn't make it any worse by pushing you. Now it's my fault, so you had an excuse to play around with this Kathy person." Realization dawned. "You've been fucking her in Jackson, then coming home and fucking me in Cheyenne! Damn you. I hope she didn't bring any communicable diseases from California."

"That's a cheap shot."

"I'm entitled to all the shots I can take. You are despicable!"

Their voices had gradually risen from murmurs to shouts.

"Shut up, you'll wake Toby," he said.

"Don't shut me up, you bastard." Jess stood in front of Karl, who still sat slumped with papers fanned around him on the floor.

"I'm sorry, sweetheart," he said.

"Don't wait till morning. Move out tonight."

His nonplussed expression looked silly. Jess stifled a laugh she knew would turn hysterical. He picked up his papers, threw some clothes in a bag, and pulled out of the driveway in the falling snow.

# 14

*Jess remembered that* Floyd always said such nice things. Her mistake was believing him.

She started seeing him right after Karl moved out. Jess was surprised to find herself attracted to another man so soon, but he was a nice-looking guy, and she was starved for attention.

Jess met him at a training course in Denver. It was always hard to find a sitter for Toby when she had to go out of town, but somehow she managed that time. She traded with other working mothers and used sitters and friends who could keep Toby several days.

Floyd Whedon was with the Forest Service. The energy boom was just starting, and oil shale looked promising. The Overthrust Belt west of Rock Springs required a regional aquifer study, which brought in people from Idaho and Utah and from other agencies for meetings. They sat in meetings and workshops all day and even ate together. At a hotel it's easy—every room is a bedroom.

Jess wondered if she had the predatory eyes of the

recently divorced—a woman looking for someone to remind her that she still existed. She felt unsteady, social skills rusty from disuse, trying for balance between aching loneliness and fear of more damage.

They had a few encounters at the Lakewood Federal Center Holiday Inn, then when she and Floyd went back to Cheyenne, he continued to buzz around her—on the phone, dropping by the office if he could find an excuse.

He knew how to make her feel good. He admired her professionalism and praised her project work on the Red Rim EMRIA Study Site near Rawlins. He also said he got a hard-on every time he thought about her body. This was balm to a woman who had been ignored for two years.

The part that made her cringe when she looked back was that she went head over heels. She acted as though she'd never been in love, never cared about anybody. She was fifteen years old and insane. She thought about Floyd constantly, obsessively. If he didn't phone every day, the usually practical and sensible Jess would go crazy.

She prepared elaborate dinners with fancy desserts and brought them over to his place. She bought fishing gear he said he wanted. She would concoct ways for them to be together, meeting him at a project site or some little town. She phoned incessantly, like a teenager with a crush. She gave Floyd presents.

She didn't *think* she was trying to buy his affection—she simply needed somebody to absorb the energy she had given to Karl. She needed to be indispensable. It pleased her to give him things, do things for him. To feel needed.

When he asked her to go with him to buy some clothes,

they drove to Fort Collins and she helped him pick out a new suit, shirts, ties, and some pants and shirts for work.

He was lanky, very tall, with a shock of snow white hair and pale blue eyes. He was fairly fit for a man his age—midforties. Younger people like Jess wore jeans all the time, but the old hands still wore khakis.

Then, for his birthday, Jess bought him more clothes, since she knew what he liked and what colors to get. When she took the presents over she color-coded his wardrobe because he was color-blind. She thought she was doing him a big favor. Everything in her life was falling apart, so she needed to manage Floyd's life.

The whole thing, she thought later, was compulsive. And she had incredible energy. Never felt tired. Got by on five or six hours of sleep a night.

The mantle had broken since the last camping trip, and Jess didn't know it, but Floyd brought a spare Coleman lantern mantle, so they had enough light to pitch the tent. He got the stove to work and they ate, very late.

They really had left too late to drive this far on a Friday night. Jess would have been happy at any of the more accessible campgrounds in the Snowies, places where she and Toby camped on weekend trips, an easy shot from Cheyenne. But Floyd had wanted to take her to his favorite place, Bennett Peak, which was a long drive off the asphalt, on a gravel road east of Saratoga, through ranch land to the North Platte River. The BLM campground was deserted in late May, and there was a risk of snow, although it was not predicted.

It was cold when the sun went down, and they kept their parkas on. They got the tent up fast, and afterward they drank coffee at the picnic table.

"It's been a long time since I've done this without Toby," said Jess. She felt guilty.

"I've never been camping with a kid. It must be very different, if you have to keep track of them every minute," Floyd said. He slipped his hand in hers.

"She's pretty responsible, but she *is* just a little girl."

"And you're a big girl," said Floyd, teasing.

"You're nice," said Jess. She squeezed his hand.

"You are more than nice. You are fabulous."

"Mnnnh."

Later, in the tent, they warmed each other up. With Floyd, making love was brief, fervent. He apologized profusely.

"It's not a problem," Jess reassured him. It felt so good to be touched, to be desired, to be talked to—sex was almost unnecessary. She thought that after a fast start they would play a while, but Floyd pulled up his sweat pants and talked about his project at work. Her replies got slower and slower until she fell asleep, a knot of tension in her lower back.

The next morning he prepared an elaborate camp breakfast for her. It felt wonderful to be taken care of—fed, loved, sheltered. He pulled on waders and a battered hat and took his fly rod into the North Platte. It was broad and shallow at this put-in place. Twice during the day other fishermen arrived and launched boats.

Jess didn't fish. Instead, after she cleaned up, she walked downstream, along tire ruts, enjoying the bright sun in the canyon of the campground; the tangle of willow, juniper, and box elder along the banks; the rabbit brush and sage; the early wildflowers—blue larkspur and bright yellow groundsel. She watched a hawk, maybe a hawk, soaring above the persistent evergreens and tilted gray rocks clinging to the mountain on the opposite side of the river.

Later they ate sandwiches, then drove to the French Creek trailhead for a hike. Floyd told her of other visits to the area, fishing trips usually. This time they did steaks on the grill and side dishes from Jess's Tupperware in the cooler. They were the only people camping overnight.

"Let's play first," Jess suggested when they went to the tent to escape mosquitoes. And she did things that other men had enjoyed. But as soon as he was erect Floyd became frantic. Was he afraid it would go away if he didn't do something fast? Jess just couldn't catch up with him, and he was off the top of the mountain while she was still climbing the foothills. Again, his apologies and her reassurance. She wondered what she was doing wrong.

They went back to Cheyenne, back to a once-a-week schedule, unless they were in the field. Most of her spare time was filled with Toby—soccer practice and Brownies until school was out. Harry Chapin sang "Cat's in the Cradle," which left a dart of regret in her heart each time she heard it.

She had to struggle to balance her work on one side of the scale and Toby and Floyd and everything else on the other. She had step increases at work and even a promotion in grade. She wondered if she could ever quit working.

Then one day Jess was forty miles into some rancher's grazing land, somewhere east of the Big Horns, and a thunderstorm would pound in from the west, purple-black clouds pouring rain on one horizon while crystal sunlight shone on the other. She waited in the cab of the truck, alone, while the thunder and rain fought their way across the scoured landscape, vivid and profound.

Then she emerged to find the sun bending a double rainbow over the mountains. She drove home stunned by the beauty as the setting sun gathered the rain clouds—ebony and silver, cobalt, rose, lavender, maroon—before it died. How could she give this freedom up?

She saw Floyd for almost a year and the whole time she was afraid that Karl would find out. She planned to use the conservatism of Wyoming lawyers and judges to get custody of Toby, and she didn't want to give Karl a chance to say "unfit parent."

Floyd was often busy, he said, and so they saw each other perhaps once a week while she was going through the divorce. She would always go to his apartment. They never went out. She preferred it that way. He was up on the latest best-sellers and movies she didn't have time to see, and he enjoyed driving to Denver for weekends.

Jess jogged in the summer and cross-country skied in the winter. She was still out in the field often enough to feel connected to the earth. In the office, indoors, with artificial lighting and no fresh air, she sometimes felt as if she were on a spaceship, completely removed from the planet.

She could sit in front of a programmable calculator and predict the amount of groundwater entering the Seminoe Reservoir two months in the future. She knew how bitter the winters could be, but still, when the weather was good, she needed to be outdoors, alone, with fresh air, with sunshine, and with no walls.

She remembered when she was pregnant with Toby, that dry summer in Casper before they moved. She drove out to Ayres State Park alone. There she waded under the natural bridge, ate a few ripe chokecherries, and spat out the oversized seeds, then followed the little stream past a grassy place with the previous weekend's picnic trash neatly piled by the trash cans.

She found a place to sit on the gravel bank beside the creek and put her feet in the water. The sun burned clear and hot despite the wind, and after a while she rolled on her side and scooped out a depression in the soft gravel beside the murmuring creek until her big belly fit into the bowl. It was cool and damp and welcoming.

Jess needed contact with what she could touch and hear and see, or she would fly off into outer space.

Toby was always up for camping, or anything outdoors, and could pack for a weekend in twenty minutes. They would come back ruddy, dirty, and happy from hikes in new places. Toby wrote up each sighting of a wild animal and tried to catch them with her Instamatic. Something about the animals—moving, alive—not on a TV screen — impressed her.

One early morning in Yellowstone, they drove along a road beside a mountain bison galloping twenty-five miles an hour. They were together for half a mile, then the buffalo veered into woods and disappeared. It took Jess's breath away.

Toby always outgrew her camp clothes—old jeans and sweatshirts—each year, but Jess's just got grubbier and more weathered as time passed.

Jess assumed that once the divorce went through she and Floyd would have a normal relationship, let it develop into something. She thought they were a perfect couple. He said he liked kids, but she never took him home to meet Toby. The signals were out; she just wasn't reading them.

She believed this was a lifelong, enduring, soul-mate relationship. She read every coincidence, every similarity as an omen that they had been meant for each other since the beginning of time. It was as though the real Jess went to sleep and this blind and naive woman ruled.

At first Jess thought Floyd was so fast in bed because he was truly wild with desire and couldn't hold back. She tried to go slow, make him please her, and he did a little, but usually after a fast few minutes it was over. She never did learn whether he couldn't help it, or was accustomed to doing it that way or was simply selfish. Later, she decided all of the above, but especially selfish.

He talked such a good game. He dreamed of the insides of her thighs, he longed to make her wild. Her breasts kept him erect at night. He tried very hard and said all the unchauvinistic things, but he had been single all his life and simply didn't understand the emotional give-and-take that most people learn in marriage, with the arguments and the shared memories and caring to soften the shell of self-absorption. You're never quite the same. Having children means you put them first and become less self-centered, in spite of yourself.

Floyd never invited her to accompany him to Denver, never offered to take her out. Jess allowed that she might have drifted along with him indefinitely if she hadn't taken the chicken soup over one Saturday, when he was sick.

Toby was at basketball practice and would go home with her friend Heather for lunch. Jess had a couple of hours, so she drove to Floyd's apartment with two freezer containers of homemade chicken soup, a box of cough drops, and a half-gallon of sherbet.

He took a long time to answer the door. He was

coughing, unshaven, and smelled stale. He wore shorts and a T-shirt and excused himself to put on a robe. Jess took her paper bag to the kitchen and put one container of soup on to heat.

Then Floyd came out and saw what she was doing. "Why are you bossing me around?" he shouted.

Jess was shocked. He had never raised his voice to her once in their ten months together. She stood there with a spoon in her hand and her mouth hanging open.

"I thought I told you to leave me alone," he said.

"I'm trying to take care of you."

"I don't need taking care of." He walked into the kitchen and turned off the burner under the soup.

"You won't go to the doctor. You won't take anything, or get a prescription. You've been in bed three days. I'm just trying to be a good friend."

Floyd put his face into hers. "Leave me alone! I don't want your caring and your manipulating and your controlling and your planning every move we make!"

"This is the first time I've heard about it." Jess's anger came alive once her dismay faded. "If you weren't happy, why didn't you give me a hint instead of saving it up to dump on me all at once. How long have you been nursing this crap?"

They had no way to get things out for discussion. No promises to "tell you how I feel" and "you have to listen," as she'd had with Kip.

"This isn't all at once. You just haven't been paying attention. I don't want you hovering over me like a nurse." He plopped down in his easy chair in a sulk.

"What else don't you want? I'd call this an overreaction to chicken soup."

"You help me buy clothes, then you buy more once you find out what I like. And try to organize every stitch I own. You tell me to see a doctor, maybe my blood sugar is low, maybe I need antidepressants, I should eat more protein. I'm fine the way I am. I don't want your advice."

"I was just trying to—"

Jess stopped. She felt as if she was being erased. She had poured all her love into this relationship and he had absorbed it. Then he decided he hated her for it and turned it back on her.

If I do all these things, you'll be happy. And I'll be what you want me to be. That was her bargain, and he had let her think it would work.

She started to say, "I'm sorry," but she didn't really feel apologetic. She was so hurt she couldn't talk. Without a word she picked up her purse and marched out.

She waited for him to phone and apologize. After a week, she phoned him. His outburst had suddenly brought her craziness down to earth. The crazy obsession died, but he was still a habit. She thought he was at least a friend.

She wanted to see him. He was busy. He didn't feel good. He had to go to Billings. After a couple of weeks, Jess finally got the message: stay out of my life.

All the things she had tried to do to make him happy turned sour. He had been Mr. Nice Guy, then he had turned into an oaf. How dare he not appreciate what she had done! He was paranoid. Jess thought she knew how to make it all better, because she would give 110 percent and it didn't matter if he gave 10 percent. She could *make* it work! If she loved him enough and did all the right things, he would learn to love her and give her what she needed.

And the harder she tried, the less he tried. It was as though the equation didn't balance, his anger didn't make sense.

Jess realized now that the whole time she was going through the divorce she needed the relationship more than Floyd did. But she didn't want to see that, not then. She had distracted herself with Floyd after Karl moved out. As long as she was legally married, Floyd would take what she gave. When she was free, when her divorce became final in November 1974, when she might expect a commitment, it was good-bye, Jess.

Once she had believed that Karl would love her, cherish her if she worked at it hard enough and gave it enough time. She had chosen him, so she had to be right. They had been a happy family. Until it had all come apart.

And she needed her relationship with Floyd to be wonderful—so she had lied to herself and said it was okay. And ignored all the things that didn't fit. Ignored all the signals that might have told her she was distorting everything.

When it finally crashed, she felt rotten.

# 15

*As an experienced hydrologist,* Jess took Ron out in the field, fed him the routine as fast as she thought he could absorb it, and added practical information to the training he had already received.

Water Resources Division collects data on ground and surface water and provides it to other agencies or whoever needs it. That was why Jess and her colleagues were out in the field—measuring floodwater, monitoring wells for the aquifer water.

She and Ron were putting in a new well. She was always disconcerted when he called her "Mrs. Stefan." Mrs. Stefan was her mother-in-law. Besides, Jess wasn't that much older—ten years. He was a hydrologic technician, taking the few science classes he needed to make hydrologist. He was bright, a fast learner, and he was fun to be with. She liked someone to lighten her, as Kip had.

Jess wondered if longing had a scent, some secret pheromone that said: I'm vulnerable, take advantage of me. She might as well have had a sign hanging around her neck. She was still aching from Karl, aching from Floyd.

Ron admired the welded rack on the roof and back of the Survey pickup. "That's cool. How'd you get a rack to hold those twenty-foot sections of casing?"

"I drew up the plans and took them to Smitty's Welding in Casper. He was real obliging. I thought he might give me a hard time because I'm a woman representing the Survey, but I explained it and he understood what we needed. I got to know some people, there in the shop, I wouldn't have known otherwise. Now we're good buddies."

"Broaden your horizons with the USGS."

Jess laughed. "Make sure the generator is stowed and the pump is tied down. We'll be on some bumpy roads today." She checked all the equipment, including the shale baskets, bentonite pellets, bottles, labels, and boxes.

Their first stop was to load casing lengths from a central cache onto the truck. They weren't heavy, just awkward. Then she drove to the drill site. She put on her yellow hard hat with her name in sticky green tape.

The drillers were already there and had gone down thirty feet. She looked at the cuttings—sand, shale, coal—and compared them to the log from the coal company. The coal company had already done core samples as part of its investigation, so she knew roughly what to expect. She wanted water samples from just above the coal seam. She told the drillers she thought they would need to go eighty feet.

At eighty feet they were still in shale, which gave the drillers a hard time because it swelled up when drilled.

"Ten more feet," she said.

"What if they go past the sandstone and into coal in that ten feet?" Ron asked.

"Then we sample the water and the coal and we drill another well."

Jess put Ron to work drilling perforations in one length of four-inch plastic casing. They got the generator off the truck. Then he connected the hand drill to the generator to perforate the casings. He dropped the drill on Jess's foot. Her boots were heavy enough to protect her toes, but her foot still ached.

"Sorry. I'm a little nervous."

"That's all right." Jess tried not to limp when she walked away.

At ninety feet Jess decided to stop drilling. Ron hurried to finish the holes, then she put a shale basket around the pipe. The drillers wrapped a heavy chain around the first length of casing and lowered it into the hole.

When the first piece was almost down, Jess glued the second piece of casing to the first and watched them lower it. The second and third pieces went smoothly, no cave-ins, then she asked Ron to do the last piece, and he got glue on himself as much as the pipe.

The drillers left by noon, and Jess and Ron stopped to eat sandwiches, sitting in the shade of the pickup. This was the part she liked. It was windy, but she had a bandanna keeping her hair out of her face. The sun warmed the clear air, and she could hear meadowlarks calling in the sagebrush.

They got the tub, concrete mix, sand, and water off the pickup. Jess measured and stirred. When Ron said, "Here, let me do that," she said, curtly: "I'm capable of mixing concrete by myself."

"Sorry."

"You were taught nice manners," Jess said. "But out here we're just Survey people. I've worked hard to prove I can do the job. I didn't mean to be rude, but you don't have to worry about me. If I can lift that one-hundred-pound sack of cement mix, I can mix it." She stirred the combination, knowing that she couldn't take too long or it would set.

A shale basket clamped to the first piece of casing flared to touch the edges of the hole. It was supposed to close off the hole to the casing so they could dump cement or dirt and cement around the casing. It would keep the cement from sealing the perforations.

They dumped in the first batch of cement, and it disappeared. The flange on the shale basket wasn't working. They shoveled dirt down the hole and mixed another batch. This time Ron mixed and they waited too long and set it in the trough. They manhandled the tub until they dumped the solidified cement out and broke it up in smaller pieces.

They got the third batch of cement down in time and they mixed another batch and filled the hole to ground level. They cut off half the protruding length of the last piece of casing, and Jess capped it to keep out animals and rain.

By then it was late afternoon, and Jess felt windburned, dry, and hungry. Her foot hurt where Ron had dropped the drill. She wiped her face with a wet bandanna and dug lotion out of her backpack for her face.

"Is that it?" asked Ron.

"No. You're not getting tired, are you?"

"No, no, of course not."

"I'm teasing. I'm tired. We have to develop the well. Get the pump."

Ron was careful with the pump, which went down

the pipe fairly easily. Jess always talked to the pump, telling it what she wanted it to do. She thought Ron looked at her funny, but it was better than swearing.

"This stuff is full of gunk," he said when the first water came out.

"Particulate matter?"

"That, too," he said and laughed.

"Keep pumping."

They pumped the well once, then waited for it to fill again. Jess calculated the volume of the casing. When they pumped again she measured the clean water from the aquifer until they had cleared three times the volume of the casing. Then Ron watched as she filled and labeled the bottles. She had prepared the labels before they left the office, and it was fairly smooth going. The bottles fit into their box, and when they were all filled Jess could pack up and drive into Medicine Bow, where they would stay until these observation wells were all in.

Ron and Jess got the generator back on the bed of the truck and packed the pump, and Ron lifted the box of water samples. When he shifted it, trying for better purchase, it tipped, he grabbed for it, and it hit the ground with a crash.

Jess stifled the desire to scream at him. She was tired, and wanted a bath and something to eat at The Virginian Hotel. She wished Ron could immediately acquire six months' experience and finesse. He apologized. If he had been smooth and never dropped anything, she never would have had any feelings about him. Jess wondered if she had been this awkward when she started. Well, somebody must have been patient with her.

She opened the box of samples. If they were contaminated, she and Ron would have to pump out more water. They were intact.

They drove to the backdoor of the post office. Jess put mailing labels on the box, and the man accepted it. It would go to the regional lab in Denver for analysis.

They trudged—dirty, sweaty, and wind-blown—into the bar. Jess ordered a beer and whatever that night's special was. She didn't even care, she was so tired.

Ron sat opposite her. Most of the other people there had already eaten and were playing the video games or pool in the back room.

She stared blankly into space.

"I'm ah, really ah sorry, I ah made it harder than it had to be," he said.

"That's all right," said Jess. She tried to smile but her face was too tired. "Everybody has a first time."

"How's your foot?"

"I don't know. I'm numb. How about you?"

"I'll probably be sore tomorrow."

"Me too. Probably."

When the food came they both ate in silence. Soft, mealy meatloaf with instant mashed potatoes, a little scorched, and brown gravy. A side dish of overcooked spinach in pot liquor. Puffy rolls and margarine in little pats. Coffee.

Jess excused herself as soon as she finished, paid, and went to her room. She scrubbed down in the shower, then refilled the tub and soaked. Her foot was swollen where Ron had dropped the drill. She even took a couple of aspirin, because everything ached.

When she answered the knock, Ron stood outside with an ice bag jury-rigged from a rubber glove—where had that come from?—and rubber bands.

"This is for your foot."

Jess was so touched that tears came to her eyes. She took the ice bag and thanked him. She woke up an hour later, put the leaking bag in the sink, and instantly fell asleep again.

As Jess recalled later, things went better after that,

Once they got the wells in they went back to Cheyenne. If it weren't for that woman Karl was living with Jess would have asked him to keep Toby in March for a couple of weeks, because that was the busy season. Toby couldn't go to Jackson and lose that much school. Jess really missed her when she was in the field, and sometimes the sitter couldn't get Toby to piano lessons or swim practice.

It's easy to get to know people when you work with them every day. Survey people practically lived together when they were out putting in wells and taking measurements. There's not much social life in those little towns, just go to the bar and have a few drinks and talk to the other people doing the same kind of work.

One night Jess drank too much. She missed Toby and she was tired. Maybe she was getting her period. She started crying and once she started, she couldn't stop. Ron tried to comfort her. He looked like a little kid who wonders where the grown-ups have gone. He finally took her by the hand and led her to her room.

He kept asking, "Are you all right?" and she just cried harder. He sat her on the bed and got a wet washcloth out of the bathroom and wiped her face. Jess finally calmed down and passed out on the bed. When she woke up the next morning she was rolled up in the blankets with her clothes on.

The next day they went about their work as usual.

Then he asked if he could drive the pickup, and she said yes and thanked him for being nice. Then he hit a hole in the road and the truck bucked so hard that the casing lengths bounced out of the rack and they had to stop and tie them on again. That night they went back to Cheyenne.

He phoned her the day after that and asked if she liked "younger men."

"I like nice men. Whatever age. You've been trying hard and you've been very nice," Jess told him.

"Could we go out?" He sounded like a teenager making his first date.

"Why don't you come over here? I like to spend time with Toby when I'm home."

So he brought a bottle of wine and a bunch of flowers and showed up wearing a coat and tie. She fed him hamburgers, which Toby said he had to cook on the grill. He took off his tie, and they played Uno with Toby until she won all their pennies. He played for blood, which Toby respected. She shared her Pop Rocks with him.

Later, Ron and Jess sat on the couch and necked. He was fun.

One night a couple of months after that, early in the winter, when she had a baby-sitter for Toby, Jess and Ron went out on a regular date for drinks and dinner, then to his apartment.

He looked as though he invented the preppy look, with his short, water-combed hair, pink button-down shirt, gold-buttoned navy blazer, rep tie, and loafers. Jess wore a new dress of royal blue silk that she knew was "her color." All the clothes, of course, came off.

"Earth to Jess, earth to Jess, come in, please."

Ron knelt at the foot of the bed, looking up at her.

Jess answered: "I'm okay, I'm okay." She opened her eyes and slowly regained full consciousness, watching him between her tits as he climbed up on top of her.

"Are you all right?" asked Ron. "I mean, you're all right from my perspective, but are you okay?"

"Yes." She swallowed and tried again. "Yes, I'm fine. I just make funny noises."

"Do you know how long we've been here?"

"No, is it late?"

"It's later than you think," in a Groucho voice. Then, "Uh-oh."

"What?" asked Jess.

"Sometime, when you were in outer space, the rubber broke. Actually, I think we wore it out. You were in outer space and I was in inner space."

"Omigod, look at the time. It *is* late."

"I never knew a woman who—never stopped."

"You must know you're a lot of fun." Jess shook herself into her bra and pulled her panties up. "Besides, it's been a long time."

"You mean next time we'll only hump for an hour?"

"Or two."

"I hope this won't change the way you treat me at work," Ron said. "I will never refer to it."

"Don't even look at me funny."

"What would you do if I told everyone?"

"Swat you down and teach you some manners." She buttoned her dress and then said, "You're doing fine. No complaints professionally or in private. Okay?" She smoothed his hair out of his eyes, pulled the electric blanket up over him, and pushed the control to HI.

There was always something maternal in her rapport with him. Jess knew that people responded to praise and encouragement, and she tried to give honest, positive feedback.

Ron had been bruised in a relationship, he confided, so she was extraprotective of his ego. His fiancée had gotten pregnant by another guy when he had been away at college.

He was careful in the office but started phoning her at home. He liked to talk dirty, and she was surprised that she liked it, too. He made puns and wisecracks, and she loosened up a little whenever she talked to him. He said he liked phone sex almost as much as the other kind, and she wondered if he got off after they hung up. She didn't like that idea.

"I give good head," he said one night when he wanted her to drive over to his place.

"So do I," Jess said. "As you know. Everybody I've ever fucked was good. Even Floyd was ardent, just too fast."

"You're lucky."

"I don't think it's just luck. People like us—"

"Sex maniacs."

"—have some secret way of identifying each other. I look at some guy and know, *know*, this one fucks. And they find me. We manage to touch, casually. We stand too close. We make a joke that's a little too raunchy. Even if we decide not to do anything, we recognize each other. There must be some chemistry that attracts us. Or magnetic fields."

That conversation drifted off in another direction, but Jess remembered it.

One crazy identifies another, and they get crazy together.

# 16

*Although she and Ron were* sexual partners, sometimes Jess did feel like his mother. He soaked up the strokes and affection and professional encouragement as if he'd been starved. Maybe he had been. But after a while she felt she was doing all the giving.

Women trade sex for intimacy. Men trade intimacy for sex. When she stopped and considered what she was doing, she felt her life was a cliche—a soap opera, suburban sex, tune in tomorrow.

She thought she was a loving person. She could give love to Toby without expecting it back. She had loved Karl a long time with very little affection in return. She thought it was generous of her—she could love people who loved her and people who didn't.

Over the years, she continued to love Kip above all. She prayed good wishes for him, hoped he was well, hoped he was happy. She didn't expect anything back from him.

But Floyd had been a taker. And Ron had his own needs. Somewhere inside him was a small, hurt child.

He tried to be affectionate, but he was so needy, he couldn't respond to Jess's emotional emptiness.

One night after they made love, Jess and Ron got dressed and she dragged kitchen chairs out onto his balcony. His apartment faced away from the street, and without street lights, they could see a few stars. Not as many as she saw when she was out on a ranch, sleeping in the pickup while a drill crew worked all night. There she could walk away from the site, away from the lights and noise, into the desert, and look up to see a million stars blur into the Milky Way, shimmering in the velvet sky.

She was always surprised that the stars were silent. They should be murmuring the music of the spheres, a grand fugue of the generosity of the universe. She and Toby always watched for shooting stars when they went camping. Thinking of Toby led her to ask Ron: "What were you like when you were little?"

"Quiet. Very quiet."

"Most little boys are loud and noisy."

"That was the only peace I knew—keeping out of the way. If they didn't notice me, they didn't scream at me."

"*They* is your parents?"

"Yes. My dad had an appliance business that was always in crisis, so he tripped out on Valium after work. Mom just drank sherry—she was a very ladylike alcoholic. When they weren't sedated, they fought. I couldn't stop the fighting, but if I kept very still, I didn't get caught up in their battles."

"Tough lesson for a little kid," said Jess. "You don't get much attention that way, though."

"Right."

Jess was silent, thinking of that silent boy.

"I was supposed to be there, but I wasn't supposed to need anything. I learned to fix breakfast for myself, if I wanted any. Then I fixed it for her. He shouted at us when he was drunk. She wept. I wondered what I was supposed to do that I didn't know.

"Little kids don't have any basis for comparison. I thought everybody's family was like ours. Nothing on TV was like this. I couldn't ask my friends. So I learned to survive by being quiet. I was quiet in school, and if I did well, I didn't attract attention, and they left me alone.

"I was on my way to being a real creep, but my friends in high school kept me going—I could blow off steam with them. They called me Chat for chatter because when I was with them I talked nonstop. Motor mouth. It was a flood of teenage talk—girls, cars, movies, teachers, ideas. I was funny, I was clever. It's almost a relief now to just relax and talk if I want to, without that rush of words I couldn't control."

Jess listened closely. What he said made sense to her. He kept trying to fill needs. Jess was the parent who listened, the undemanding lover, the understanding friend.

Everything Ron said had a double meaning. He breathed puns. He said it was because in his family everything meant something else. When Mother had a headache it meant she was drunk. When she was sick to her stomach, that was a hangover. Daddy was "relaxing." And when Ron got older, in his teens, he could say things disguised in puns and jokes that he couldn't say otherwise.

He buried his resentment and anger under the jokes. His parents never physically abused him, they just ignored him and let him grow up alone. So he was insecure, because he didn't learn what normal kids learn—what the limits were, how much you can expect of people.

Jess thought he would always look for what he didn't get from his parents. She tried to give it, then one day *she* needed help—because she was burned out from work and tired. She had been in the field a lot that summer. She needed some help at the house and someone to lean on for a while but all he ever really did was bring her a cold washcloth for her head.

She had been telling herself it was wonderful, exciting, romantic—an older woman, younger man. Really with it, as an article in *Time* magazine had said about older women who were, gosh! over forty. Actually, Jess was only thirty-five. But when she quit giving constantly, Ron just faded away and eventually found someone else.

That was when she noticed that all the men in her life left. And it all felt bad except Kip. Maybe she needed to look at what she was doing. Or talk to Kip. Karl could try to take Toby away if he found out she was sleeping around. Plus, Toby would catch on, and Jess didn't want her daughter to think it was okay to be so irresponsible.

One night, as she drove home from a meeting at the university, the blank stretch of interstate from Laramie to Cheyenne emptied her mind—the horizontal landscape, picturesque vistas of distant mountains, dark specks of grazing cattle, dim sunset behind banked clouds. In a half-trance induced by driving, a memory of Kip took form.

One night, early on, clothes tossed all over the room, they had stood naked beside her bed.

"Don't look so worried," he had said and smiled. She was reassured. His smile was safety.

"I've never felt like this," she said.

Kip kissed her. What was different about his kisses, those long, teasing kisses that he never rushed? He knew she loved them. He pushed her backward. She fell, fell. The bed came up, the cotton spread against her back. Kip knelt and found her secret places.

"Do you really like to do that?" she had asked, between gasps.

"You bet I do."

She grasped the ribbed spread and was gone. Explosions, waves. She cried out, taut with pleasure.

He laughed and scooted them both into the center of the bed. She tasted herself hot and salty on his lips. He was doing something else and she was out of her head, couldn't think, couldn't stop. She opened her eyes.

His face over her, smiling, a fierce look in his eyes, a quick kiss, then his body with hers, warm and full. Another wave swept her away.

When it was over, Kip rolled off and got under the spread, but she couldn't move. She tried to sit up, but fell back onto the bed. She couldn't open her eyes, couldn't lift her head. They talked about how they felt, and Kip told her about something he wanted to work on.

"You're shivering," he said and noticed that she was goosebumped.

"I'm cold."

"It's my job to get you warm." He got up and found a blanket, since she couldn't seem to move. Then he held her.

What was different about Kip? He wasn't a child who needed her to mother him. He wasn't self-centered, like Floyd, who wanted to get off and then quit. Kip was a friend. He was a gift—like light, like rain.

She knew that if she were ever in trouble, no matter how long it had been since they had seen each other, she could ask for help and he would give it. She could tell him her secrets and be forgiven.

They had told each other fantasies and dreams, and she knew that part of him better than she had ever known Karl. They had been young, selfish, committed to their own lives. She had no secrets from him. He had always accepted her as she was. Maybe that was what love felt like.

---

But when Ron left, Jess immediately began thinking of a new lover. She knew she should stop, but the energy was addicting—she got swept up in the excitement of it. Making arrangements, anticipating, keeping secrets, playing a role. And she always found another sex junkie who was mainlining that same excitement, getting off on the *event*. What fantasy was the other guy acting out? "Being in love" is an altered state. She was crazy, a different person. One she didn't like.

The last time scared Jess because it came close to Toby, the one person Jess loved most.

She had gone to a party out at a ranch. Lots of people at a cookout. They'd dug a pit to barbecue the meat. A fund-raiser for some politician. Several people from the office were there, and people she knew from other contexts—PTA parents, basketball mommies. There were even a couple of newspaper people. It was almost a photo op—perfect cross section of middle class voters. The hostess wore a reproduction dress, leg o'mutton sleeves and ball fringe; the host looked like he had stepped out of a Ralph Lauren ad. And there were officers from Francis E. Warren Air Force Base.

Jess met Lieutenant Colonel Byron Taafe at the barbecue. They found adjacent chairs under an awning, where they sat and made small talk as they ate barbecued beef, cole slaw, beans, and potato salad. He was attractive in the spit-and-polish way military men always are, even when they wear an Izod shirt, Levis, and Justin boots.

She flirted a little, and he responded. She left it at that and went to find a friend from the PTA to chat with before she left. That friend was in a group laughing at wisecracks from the candidate.

Byron followed her and stood on the fringes of the group, listening, pleasant. Eventually, he worked his way over to Jess and asked if he could take her home, "when she was ready."

Jess looked at him, measuring him, wondering what it would be like to get naked with him. The veins stood out on his muscular arms. He had a cute butt, long legs, and big hands—the biggest hands Jess had noticed in a long time. And they were groomed, but scarred. She wondered what had happened to them.

She had her own car and agreed to go to his apartment, where they had sex quick and hard. Both of them had been hungry. The second time she expected slower, gentler sex, with more play and tenderness, but it was almost brutal. Another land speed record. It bothered her that she liked it—she was so aroused that only pleasure registered. Till afterward. She was shaky when she got back in her car.

She always thought that the only harm done was to herself, but this time she went deeper into a part of herself she hadn't seen before.

They saw each other as often as Jess could manage. Finding baby-sitters was a constant problem. And she always thought she had missed something by working while Toby grew up, so she tried to be there when she wasn't working. She would tire of the constant responsibility and wish for a spouse, housemate, somebody to dump Toby on so she could have a minute alone. Then she would swing to the other extreme of feeling guilty because she had yearned for freedom.

Most of the time she went through the daily routine without thinking. She didn't try to make every moment with Toby meaningful, but she answered questions. Toby could watch afternoon kids' TV shows alone, but if there was something she wanted to watch after dinner, they would sit on the couch together.

Jess rubbed Toby's back or brushed her blond hair, which had darkened from the pale baby tow to a color closer to Jess's. Toby chattered about school, complaining of the demands on fourth graders. They argued about what clothes she would wear and whether she needed a bath and when she could have a Walkman and whether she'd buy tapes from her allowance and who was going to clean up after she made cookies.

Then, when she was bathed and had her pajamas on and teeth brushed, Jess read to her. Jess always tried to find books at the library that Toby could read but that wouldn't be too easy. *The Giving Tree*, or *Amelia Bedelia*. She outlawed *Green Eggs and Ham* when she got sick of Dr. Seuss rhymes. Toby grew up without Winnie the Pooh, because it made Jess want to puke.

But for the first two weeks after Jess met Byron Taafe she ignored Toby and went to Byron Taafe's house every night, either after work or later, even though Toby missed one softball practice.

He was balding and ultra-clean-cut, his shoulders permanently braced. He worked out and had hard muscle under his dry, somewhat aging skin. Jess had at first guessed he was her age, but the army had moved him to so many places, it seemed he should be much older. He talked about 'Nam, about Germany, about Turkey, about Korea, and about Omaha, SAC headquarters. What Byron did exactly he wouldn't discuss, but Jess thought it must have to do with missiles or silos, since Warren was a SAC base.

"I want to try something special," he said on the second or third night. His voice was soft and husky when he was alone with her. He was gentle, persistent.

"Like what?" asked Jess.

He reached into the night table and brought out a handful of bright silk scarves. Jess still didn't catch on.

"Let me tie you up," he said. He wasn't demanding or whining. It was a straightforward request.

"I don't like that," she said quickly.

"I'll make a loop that you can get out of any time," he said. He smiled and spoke softly and tied a big loop of silk and slipped it over her hand. He was reassuring and said he would stop the instant she wanted him to. And it seemed perfectly reasonable to try it. It might be fun, and he was perfectly safe, wasn't he?

He wanted to try other things she turned down—she wasn't into the games he liked. She agreed to blindfold him with one of the silk scarves, and this excited him. Maybe it was just the novelty of the forbidden, but she saw in herself possibilities she didn't like. He left bruises and scratches that she didn't find till later. She began to acknowledge a dark shadow in herself.

Byron wanted to do it on the floor, standing, on the kitchen counter, in the shower. It was interesting to experiment, and then Jess found herself looking forward to his quirks for a bigger turn-on.

"Let's try it with this," Byron once suggested. He had a riding crop on the night table. He knelt over her, his face in shadow, dim light from the hall behind him.

"That makes me feel funny. I pass."

He shrugged and apparently forgot it, but the next time and the time after that, he brought it up. He offered to use it on her, but she refused that, too. He wanted a second woman. Or a second man.

What astounded Jess was that each new suggestion was harder to refuse. She thought she was predictable and ordinary in this, as in the rest of her life, but she was afraid he would wear her down and she would eventually do everything he wanted, feel degraded, but do it anyway.

The third weekend after they met, when they had been together nearly every night, Jess invited Byron to her house for dinner. She and Toby made lasagna, and Toby set the table with the good china and stemmed glasses. Byron was complimentary and joked in the heavy-handed way of adults who aren't around children often. Afterward, Jess and Byron cleaned up the kitchen and then sat in the living room and drank the last of the wine while Toby watched Bob Newhart and Carol Burnett on TV in the family room.

When Toby fell asleep, Byron and Jess went to Jess's room. They were quiet but active. She liked falling asleep with another warm body in the bed.

Jess woke up about three A.M. and went into the hall to go to the bathroom. Byron was standing at Toby's door, looking in at the sleeping child. A cold shaft of fear dropped from Jess's brain down her spine and turned her belly to ice. What was he doing at Toby's door? She was suddenly terrified that he might do something to Toby. He liked feigned violence; maybe he liked real violence. She really did not know him very well out of bed.

She forced her voice to sound normal. "Can't sleep?" What was he looking at?

"Just getting a drink." His voice was husky, as it always was. "I was checking on Toby."

That one innocuous sentence threw Jess into a panic. Now anything sounded sinister.

"Would you mind leaving before Toby gets up?" she asked. She cleared her throat. "I don't know how I'd explain it to her if you were here in the morning."

"Sure. Shall I go now?"

She shrugged.

Byron dressed, and she forced herself to kiss him good-bye at the door, as she normally did. She almost cringed.

She stopped seeing him, cold. He phoned every night. First he was ingratiating, then demanding. He drove past her house every evening. She told the police what was happening, and they said something had to happen before she could file a complaint. But she noticed that police cars patrolled her street more often.

One night she picked up the phone and heard his husky, seductive voice.

"I'm coming to your house," the purring voice threatened. He paused, but she was mute with fear. He continued: "I know where your patio door is, know how to break into your bedroom, ground floor, like Toby's . . ." The voice was as soft as ever and the absence of emotion in it chilled Jess more than shouts would have.

Later that night he came to the door. Jess did not answer.

"I know you're in there! I can break in!" He scarcely raised his voice.

Toby was terrified. Jess held her until Byron stopped pounding, then she sat and read to Toby until the little girl fell asleep.

When the phone rang Jess knew who it was.

"I want you," Byron said.

"Please leave me alone." The phone was sweaty in her hand. "If you don't, my lawyer will get a restraining order to keep you away from me."

"I haven't done anything."

"Stay away from me."

"I'll tell your little girl."

That froze her to her core. She wasn't afraid of what he might tell Toby, but she realized in a flash of fear that he could find out where Toby went to school. Toby would be in danger!

"You're ashamed," Byron taunted.

Jess hung up.

Later that night, after hours of feeling terrorized, she dozed. She awakened when she heard someone try the front door. She shot up in bed, tried to remember if she had put the dowel in the patio door. Her heart pounded. She listened. He tried the patio door, but it didn't slide, so she must have remembered. She slid out of bed and went to the window. Byron's Saab was parked outside.

She phoned the police to report a prowler, but Byron had left before the police arrived. She did not sleep until dawn.

Jess was afraid of him. She had seen her own darkness and she feared his. She was most afraid for Toby.

She kept her daughter home from school the next day and phoned a lawyer. Then she called Byron.

"Stay away from me," Jess said. "In every way. I know you were here last night. I bought a gun."

"I'm not afraid of you," he said. "If I want something, I take it." His seductive voice was quiet, almost offhand. The gentle tone didn't match the words.

Slowly, deliberately, she said, "Never threaten me. My lawyer is talking to your superiors. If you don't leave me alone, I'll make you sorry. In the ugliest ways I can. Do you understand?" The phone trembled in her hand, but her voice stayed steady.

There was silence on the line. Jess let it build. After two full minutes, which seemed like an hour, he said, "Very well. Good-bye."

Jess hung up. The handset slipped off the cradle because she was shaking, and she picked it up and had to use two hands to get it on the cradle. She went to the bathroom to wash her face and calm down, but once she was there she vomited in convulsive spasms. She had a piercing headache behind her eyes. That evening she read to Toby, then lay awake on her bed. The revolver lay on her nightstand. She was afraid of it, but knew how to use it. She scarcely slept.

A week later the lawyer reported that Byron had been transferred to a training unit in Omaha.

# 17

*As soon as Jess was sure* Byron wasn't coming back, she phoned Kip. The school year was almost over, and Toby would spend June with her father in Jackson Hole.

"I need to talk to someone I can trust," she said to Kip.

He told her the date his photo workshop ended at Chico Hot Springs. He took the participants for a soak in the hot springs and good food, after they backpacked and took pictures in one of the wilderness areas of Yellowstone Park, thirty miles south.

"I need to talk, but I'm counting on you to tell me how you feel," she said.

"And you have to listen," he reminded her.

"I keep messing myself up, making the same mistakes."

"I can't do magic," he said.

"Hope springs," she said.

When they saw each other it was as though they had just said good-bye last week, not ten years ago in Santa

Fe, not three years ago when Kip and Megan had stopped in Cheyenne on a trip. And they talked through a late lunch and a drink in the bar and finally, when she couldn't stand it another moment, Jess asked, and of course he said yes.

It always worked.

From the first night, when he had showed up at her door in Casper. After all these years.

Whenever Jess spent ten minutes with Kip, she wanted to make love. He did, too, it turned out. The years fell away, all their responsibilities disappeared for the moments they were together. He remembered how sensitive her breasts were. "That's my girl," he said. And she was soaring and he joined her and they did the things they did when they were kids and new things they had learned since.

"Do you like that?" he asked.

"Especially that," Jess gasped. And the world exploded again. "Come back." She sighed.

And they came together again. Then she found herself sucking his tiny nipples hidden in chest hair, listening to him moan. His hands in her hair tugged and kneaded like a cat on a cushion. He kissed her mouth, her breasts, kissed his way down and she fell off the mountain, fell and fell. She was helpless. He ignored her pleas to stop, kept finding new places to pleasure until surrender was total. Then they collapsed, spent, still rocking in the waves.

Jess lay in Kip's arms in the high, old-fashioned bed and wept. Out the window of the hotel room she could see the Paradise Valley sunset beyond the mountains to the west. Night gathered indigo clouds, turned the sky crimson, amethyst, plum, garnet, and stole the light away. The bedspread flung over the foot of the bed, clothes thrown on the floor. Kip murmured sounds that weren't words and held her close as she cried.

She craved his skin, glued to hers. She drank the deep timbre of his voice. She put her hand into his black hair, felt its softness. She breathed the smell of fresh sweat and sex from him. She couldn't take in enough of him.

"I've messed up so badly," she said and shook with tears of remorse. "And I'm trying to mess you up."

"No, no," Kip murmured. He shifted to free one hand, then stroked her hair out of her face, but she couldn't look him in the eyes. She buried her face in his neck. She thought she would drown in tears, go under where she couldn't breathe, couldn't think.

They eased down in the bed and Kip pulled the sheet over them. He pushed the pillows into place behind them and settled back with her in his arms. She remembered that he usually fell asleep for a couple of minutes afterward, but before she could tell him this, she was asleep.

When she woke up, it was dark out. She pulled clothes on for the trip down the hall to the bathroom. Kip's room was in the old building at Chico Hot Springs, built in 1900, electricity and plumbing added later. It was only eleven-thirty, and she could hear music from the bar on the first floor.

She slid back in beside him and lay there, awake in the dark, counting her sins until she drifted to sleep again.

In the morning, Kip got up, breakfasted with his workshop students and told them good-bye. He came back to the room and together they went down to the pool. He swam laps in the cooler part for a while, then joined her in the shade, where she sat, back to the hot water pipe. She was buoyant in the mineral water and so relaxed she thought she would dissolve.

She owed Kip an explanation.

On their way back upstairs, he stopped at the desk and extended his reservation. He phoned Megan's office and left a message that he would be gone an extra day.

"Tell me what's wrong," said Kip when they got back to the room. He sat in the slipcovered chair, one leg over the arm. He put his hand down beside the chair, then smiled and said, "I'm used to the dog." He was still thin and boyish, but the squint lines around his eyes were deeper and his hair was shot with silver. He had a fresh, high-altitude sunburn over a deep tan.

Jess climbed up on the bed and arranged the pillows for a backrest.

"I can't seem to stop making the same mistake." She wasn't going to cry. She had cried last night. Even Kip would grow weary of tears. She was sick of them. But she just couldn't seem to stop them.

"Which is?"

"With men, picking the wrong ones. Not you! Just since the divorce. I need to get myself straightened out. I can't keep on like this."

"Did you seek professional help, as Ann Landers says?" Kip asked. "I don't mean to turn you off, but it might help."

"My therapist has me going back to my childhood, which I suppose is necessary, but it takes a long time and I feel like I'm coming apart right now."

"Talk to me."

Jess told Kip about Floyd, Ron, and Byron. About the chicken soup and dropping the drill and the heart-stopping night Byron tried to break into her house. She felt she had to tell him everything, even if she bored him. Even if she disgusted him.

She had to sort it out for herself. She needed his acceptance. When she was afraid that his patience was wearing, she asked about his life, and he told her about Aquilino and Megan's asthma. They drove into Livingston for lunch and a visit to Sax & Fry, a great bookstore, then they talked through the long afternoon.

Kip was jealous of Jess's lovers, although he had no right to be. He remembered that "earth-to-Jess" feeling —when she was out of her mind. The reasonable, calm, practical woman disappeared.

Spending time with a healthy woman felt to him like a shot of adrenaline. He was so used to thinking of Megan's limitations and worrying that she would overextend herself, he hadn't realized how relaxed he could be with Jess. Her energy was prodigious. He got a little weary listening to her work her way through it all, but knew he only needed to let her know she was okay.

Jess wore a knit shirt with a bandanna scarf and a full denim skirt. He would want her no matter how she looked, but she looked good. Everyone dressed Western from Shepler's or Tourist from the L. L. Bean catalog these days.

Kip found being with her too much to resist. He wanted to make love, and that blotted out Megan and his duty and even Jess's need for support and help. He thought about her body—firm under the softness. Her breasts were fuller, and he remembered her nursing Toby at the restaurant in Santa Fe. Her hair was shoulder length, cut simply, shades darker than he remembered.

She cried and talked herself out, and his responses reflected what she said like a mirror held at a different angle. It was hard for him to listen to her talk about other men. Finally, she worked her way back to the real pain—the divorce and Karl. For two years, through his depression, when he ignored her, Karl's silence was abuse. The unspoken message: you aren't worth talking to, you have nothing I want to hear. When Karl acted as though he didn't like her, much less love her, she became vulnerable to whatever guy paid her any attention.

"Then Karl left and I missed him and felt sorry for myself and thought, 'What a waste of my best years,' and it's not fair and I really want good things for him even if it isn't me and I can't do this alone. And, and, and."

"Everybody needs to be somebody's something," Kip said.

"What?" she asked.

"Rock lyric, from an old Jackson Browne song."

Jess felt as if she had taken a direct hit in the solar plexus. She bent over, couldn't catch her breath.

"Are you all right?" Kip asked.

"Say that again."

"Everybody needs to be somebody's something."

Jess tried to fend off the idea, but it had already gone home. "When I wasn't Karl's wife, I needed to be Floyd's something, Ron's mama. Byron's victim. God that hurts."

"Sorry."

"No. Sometimes the heart murmurs comfort, and sometimes it says what I need to hear. Oh God. I should have seen it coming." The tears started again, and Jess grabbed her purse for tissues. The last of her mascara washed away. She would have to switch to waterproof.

She had been angry and hurt because of what Karl and the others had done, blaming them for her misery.

When she looked at it from Kip's perspective, she could see that it was her own weakness.

She had lied to herself that her marriage was okay. Sure, lots of people spent time apart. She and Karl were so solid that strain of separation couldn't shake their marriage. She knew best what Karl needed, and she would give it. She believed that Karl would love her, cherish her if she worked hard enough and gave it enough time. She chose him, so it must be right. They were a happy family.

Until it all came apart.

So she lied to herself and said that the affairs were okay. And ignored all the things that didn't fit. Ignored all the signals that might have told her she was distorting what happened.

"I believed it was wonderful," she said.

"Well, nobody ever died of chagrin," said Kip. He got up and patted her shoulder. "Speaking of giving and taking, I can't stand to see you on that bed alone."

Every time Kip looked directly in her eyes, his face broke into a wide smile. His eyes lit up and he seemed genuinely happy to see her. It had been a long time since anybody had smiled just because she was there. She was surprised at how powerful his smile was.

"I look awful," Jess wailed through the tissue.

"Just your face."

"Thanks a lot!"

But she grabbed him and buried her face in his belly. His belt buckle scratched her chin. In a few moments she released him from the tummy hug and he stopped her tears and they floated on the raft of the big old bed and he wouldn't let her drown for a while.

° ° °

That night they ate at the best restaurant in a hundred miles. Movie stars who lived in the area were supposed to patronize the place, but Jess didn't see Peter Fonda or Jeff Bridges there.

Jess felt wonderful. After a long stretch of abstinence since Byron Taafe, her skin hunger was satisfied. She no longer jumped each time Kip touched her, she no longer wanted to hang on him every moment. They drank coffee and cognac, and then they walked down the straight road past the modern motel building at the resort, squinting in the high country sunset.

"It must be hard to take," Jess said. "Megan's situation."

"I think I should be noble and brave, and all I want to do is keep her healthy. I want to scream." Kip felt his jaw tighten.

"Go ahead."

He twisted his mouth in a bitter smile.

"You're being hard on yourself," Jess said. "comparing your jealousy to a two-year-old's tantrum when Mommy brings home a new baby. It's more than that. Some men resent their own children without knowing what it is—jealousy. The wife can do something normal —'Not tonight, honey, I've been running car pools all day'—and he takes it wrong. We all have an empty place at the core, we don't know why, and we're scared of it. And when we get too close, we drink or do drugs or start fights or work too hard."

"Or have affairs."

"Ouch. Yes. To cover the scare. You're smart enough to name it and live with it. And you haven't done anything dumb to cover it or pretend you don't feel anything."

They walked back to the resort, then up the hill behind the buildings as they talked. Somewhere up there Jess thought there was a lake.

"I feel like hell," Kip admitted.

"Can you feel bad without exploding? Do you have a relief valve?"

"I go fishing."

"How do you keep from burning out at work?" she asked.

"I take these workshops out. Try to show how beautiful the world is, so people don't ruin it. Not really a do-gooder, but taking pictures is my thing." He thought for a moment. "I go back to the photo workshop every year, maybe help some kid along."

Kip thought of the memories that came without summons, of Jess, of them, of the brief time they'd spent together.

Did they keep him from exploding? They built a charge of longing which he tried to rechannel with Megan. Was that wrong?

They walked back in the growing dark.

"Weren't we in love once?" he asked.

"We were in something," she answered. "Lust, for sure. Mutual support. God, I wanted you to succeed and I knew you'd leave when you did."

"You made sure I ate and got enough sleep and stayed warm. And my cameras kept working. You supported me."

"We supported each other," said Jess. "We were truly close. That was what I was reaching for with Floyd and the others. I finally noticed I wasn't getting what I wanted. Just sex. No companionship, no caring."

They took drinks from the bar up to their room.

"When we were together," said Kip, "we were so young we didn't know what roles we wanted to play. Neither of us dumped the other, we just made a choice. We could work things out—we still are—so we could stay friends." He put his drink on the nightstand and turned to embrace her.

"You have a different relationship with Megan," Jess said.

Kip could smell her hair and feel her warmth through her shirt. He wondered if he could hear the hum of her energy.

"I remember our times together more vividly than all the hundreds of times with Megan."

"Oh, Kip." Her voice, full of emotion, doubled him over. Jess held him as he struggled for breath. He felt his face convulse and waited till he could see again. He grabbed her. Her fervent response made it hard to breathe. She could hold him up. With Jess he could be weak.

"Megan's your wife," said Jess. "It's love and duty and a lot of things that you can't walk away from. And she'll get worse?"

"Probably."

"And you're all she has?"

"Yes."

"And you can't abandon her when she needs you."

"No."

"Because you love her."

"Yes."

Later, they lay in silence, absorbing the other's affection, storing comfort in their bodies.

Kip wondered what was the right thing to say to Jess. "You haven't confessed anything I can't forgive," he said. "You're mad at yourself for being foolish. You're blaming yourself—what's wrong with me that I had these bad affairs. You're thinking you should have known better."

"Sometimes," Jess said, "I think I will never drain the

anger. It scares me. If I ever let it go, I would destroy the world."

"Can you find a safe place to let it out?"

Jess nodded. "My shrink." She thought. "I have work, I have Toby, I have the rest of my life—" She paused again to think, then with a quiet voice she said, "I can't believe I'll spend the rest of my life single."

Kip said nothing. She looked bleak, brave, and her face was so sad that he couldn't look at it. For all his problems, at least he wasn't alone.

"But I can," she concluded, "if that's the way it is."

"Don't expect Toby to prop you up. She'll grow up and be gone sooner or later."

"Oh Kip! I can be strong and take myself in hand and do what I have to do, but I don't think I can live without you." She threw her arms around him. "I wish I didn't love you! I don't want this to be all we'll ever have. After you leave, I'll miss you more than ever."

Kip knew he would pay the price, too, in memories so vivid he got lost in them, memories so indelible he couldn't erase them, memories so warm he was glad he couldn't.

They held each other and made sounds that weren't words, but murmurs of the heart, until her tears stopped. Comforted and comforting, they slept.

The next morning they swam, showered at the pool, and returned to the room.

Kip shaved as Jess packed. "Will you be all right?" he asked over the shaver's motor.

"Will you?" Jess felt purposeful for the first time in a while. She had done something positive for herself.

"Yes," he said, softly, sorrowfully.

"It would be very easy for us to arrange this kind of thing occasionally." Jess had to get this issue out on the table.

"I thought of it," he admitted. "But—"

"Yes, there's that *but*—"

"We can't keep doing this," he said. "If we use each other for comfort we won't do what we have to do."

Jess nodded and pushed the last item into the corner of her bag. "I want to know your phone number, where you live, where you work. But I won't call you, I won't find you again. I need to know I can, though."

"Any time," Kip said.

Jess stopped and considered what she had just said. "You've always got a friend in Cheyenne. I'll send Christmas cards." She glanced over the unmade bed and the dirty clothes and Kip's backpacking gear stacked against the wall. "You're not hurt?"

"No. I know what you're saying. I won't use you to avoid my problems, either." He kept his head down and didn't look at her.

"I don't want to believe I'll never see you again." Jess lay down on the side of the bed and buried her face in the sheet.

"Don't think about it," Kip said. He sat beside her with one arm around her shoulders.

"We both have responsibilities," she told the sheet. "I have Toby, my work. I was really good at taking care of Karl and the others, so if I use that energy on myself, I should be able to get it together. And definitely do it celibate. I can't be a whole person in a relationship until I'm okay alone."

Kip knew that if he didn't leave now, he couldn't do it at all. He stood and opened his arms. "One last hug?" She got up and wrapped her arms around his thin, hard back, smelled his sweet neck just inside his collar, put her hand in his soft hair. She felt his ragged breath.

He pulled her close. "It's hard to know this is all we'll have."

Kip's breath was warm in her hair, and he held her so tightly she ached. She knew his body, a poem she memorized when she was young. She knew the vibration of his voice, how his kisses tasted, his hand span. She wanted to remember it exactly, so that when she thought of him, he would come back sharp and clear, like one of his photographs.

"Think of me sometimes," she said.

"I love you."

Kip left first, making two trips to his Cherokee with his cameras and backpacking gear. Jess waited until she saw his car pull down the long, straight road away from Chico, then she carried her bags down to her car. She would pick up Toby in Jackson and go back to her life. It would be awful, and difficult, and wonderful.

# 18

*Jess couldn't remember* a time when Paul Storms hadn't been around. She had known him since she was first assigned to the Casper office. He was senior hydrologist in charge of technicians.

She had gone to his house for Thanksgiving dinner that awful first November when Kip left. She remembered cuddling Paul's little boy, Jonathan, between courses in the dinner. Paul's wife, Mil, was a beautiful blond woman whom Paul had met at the University of Minnesota. She taught home economics in Casper high schools before they had children.

Besides Jonathan, Paul and Mil had Alan and Elisa, then Heather. Paul transferred to the Cheyenne office the year before Jess, and she always looked to him, as to an older brother, for information and advice outside the office as well as in. Mil was a perfect housekeeper and mother, and she set a standard Jess never achieved.

Mil had stayed home until all the kids were in school all day. The she had gone back to teaching but found that kids all day *and* all night were too much. So she'd opened a shop and sold crafts supplies and macramé rope, then after much agonizing, she and Paul had borrowed a lot of money so she could open a furniture store downtown, with full decorating services and accessories.

All the government employees, air force base personnel, and people moving in during the energy boom in the seventies and eighties made the store a success. In fact, Mil earned much more than Paul's salary at USGS, which made it easier in some ways when she decided to divorce Paul and marry a widower who owned a ranch east of Hanna on the Medicine Bow River. Jess had collected water samples from his wells.

After being a solid shoulder for Jess, Paul needed Jess's ear for a couple of years while his ex-wife and the rancher worked out where they would live—Cheyenne during the week, ranch on weekends—and who would get the kids. Paul kept them during the school year so the kids wouldn't miss sports, extracurricular activities, and their social life. Then she took them for the summer, when they wanted to be outdoors every day. Since Paul was in the field more during the summer, it worked out all right.

Jess was a good friend to Paul, and they drank many cups of coffee in the lunchroom at the office, and at the pancake house while he tried to figure out what had happened to his life. Jess encouraged him to continue going to St. Mark's Episcopal so he could socialize with the single women in the congregation. This turned out to be good for Paul, who found companionship this way. He and these women had religion in common, and certainly he was attractive. He had gone gray but stayed stocky and fit, and he had the kind of brown-green eyes that changed colors.

During 1977–78 Paul and Jess were both vestrymen

and worked on the finance committee at St. Mark's. He would pick her up, since they lived in the same subdivision, to go to the old church downtown for their monthly committee meeting. Afterward, they usually stopped for a beer at the Mayflower, an old style cowboy bar before it got cleaned up for tourists and yuppies.

"How do you talk to a teenage girl who gets testy and picks on her brothers just before she gets her periods?" Paul asked her one evening at the bar.

"Give it a name, the Curse of the Vampire," Jess said and giggled, "or something like that, and some time when she's not on the rampage, tell her what you've observed and tell her you understand where she's coming from, but she's hard to live with."

"Will that work?"

"Worth trying. I'm like Dear Abby—no guarantees, I just give advice." Jess finished off her glass of draft beer and stopped cold. "My God," she said, "One of these days I'll have to deal with that with Toby."

"Right now I feel like the keeper in a zoo where these enormous animals make noise, mess things up, and eat all the time."

"That sounds about right."

"I mean, they're good kids, and they all have chores, but sometimes when the music is on and Alan and Jon are wrestling, the whole house rocks."

"I guess I shouldn't complain about all the noise one little girl can make."

Paul shook his head. "Wait till you hear four."

"How do you stand it?"

"I go back in the kitchen after they clean up. As long as they do homework and keep their grades up, I'm glad they're home. At least I know what they're doing. Talking on the telephone and arguing about who's been on too long and whose turn it is. Bouncing the basketball in the driveway for two hours running. Ka-thump, ka-thump." He laughed. "That basket is a magnet. Kids come from all over the northeast end of town. They wore out one backboard and I replaced it with a plastic one. Then they eat a second dinner—all junk food." He paused. "And on the weekends when they're gone it's so quiet I can hardly stand it."

"When I get stretched too thin with car pools and lessons and practice and this committee, I remind myself—this is my life, this is *it*. Enjoy it." Jess smiled at how simple her new philosophy sounded.

"Me, too. When I remember. I usually get sunk in it and forget that someday they'll all be gone. It'll take me, Mil's store, and the ranch to get them all through college."

"That's a generous attitude. You don't seem bitter any more."

"It's been a couple of years. The things that cut so deep at first—well, I've gotten used to them. We've worked out ways to take care of the kids. The kids are great. They talk about it, complain, work it out for themselves. But—"

"Which 'but' is that?" Jess sat back in the booth and waited while Paul ordered another round.

"But I miss being married."

"You don't miss Mil?" she asked.

"It's funny, but I don't. We'd gotten half-separated before the divorce. She was doing her thing."

"I certainly was used to Karl being gone, but after the divorce, it was different. I was doing some crazy stuff."

"You got yourself together by the time I got divorced."

"Thanks."

"I miss the other body in the bed," said Paul. He looked at her funny. Jess felt uncomfortable.

"I miss her smells, not just perfume, but her. I guess that's crude."

"No, I know what you mean. The physical presence of somebody breathing next to you."

Paul nodded.

"I miss that, too," she went on. "Sharing dinner, whatever it is—hamburgers, macaroni and cheese. Knowing there's somebody to listen to what you have to say."

"Or at least care if you show up."

"I leave messages, with the sitter, with the office, so that if I drop dead thirty miles out on somebody's ranch, I would be missed. Sooner or later."

"I'd miss you," Paul said. Very seriously.

Jess looked at him carefully. His eyes were big and deep, and she realized he meant it—and not just miss her, a coworker and committee member and car pool driver, but her, the person.

"Paul?"

"I'm trying to get serious and I'm not very smooth."

"Don't ruin a great friendship." Jess felt flustered and hot and wondered why it had taken her so long to catch on. She squirmed and wanted to be somewhere else.

"I won't, if you want me to stop."

"Yes. Stop." She blew her nose, sipped beer, and said, "I just never thought of you, of us—you were out of reach for me. I'll have to think about this. Not that you're not attractive—but I'm programmed to think Paul equals brother, or Paul equals friend."

"Try Paul equals lover."

• • •

It was a roller coaster for twelve years in Paul's house, Storms Zoo, with five kids and two adults. Jess never had enough time. She hadn't known how hard she could work, but when it was most hectic, there was Paul, sharing it. Maybe just a glance exchanged over children's heads, or a pat on the fanny when she stood at the stove. It was the sweet weight of his arm on her waist when they finally settled in for sleep.

They had to plot to find time alone, preferably when the kids were busy elsewhere or sleeping, but they found it. Paul's wedding present to her was a king size bed and two down comforters and two sets of pillows, firm and soft. He put in good reading lights. They broke the bed in well the first time the kids, including Toby, all went to the ranch.

Their honeymoon was delayed, then each summer they had time, in spite of work in the field, to get to know each other again, to become lovers again. This wasn't the high-energy youthful spontaneity of Kip, or the powerful chemistry of Karl, or the compulsive, addictive affairs, but a meeting of good friends, business partners, continuing lovers.

Paul respected her, and there was always a give-and-take about who did what. Jess did almost the same work, was raising the same kids. Paul was liberated, because there was no way to keep up with all the work and fun of raising kids otherwise. What he and Jess loved most was watching them grow up.

Soon Jonathan left for college. Toby and Heather were the same age, and best friends already, and they always shared a room. Schedules changed—basketball practice and cheerleading, school paper, class trips, piano lessons. Money-raising car washes.

The boys went from men's smalls to men's large so

fast that Jess got hand-me-ups—their scarcely worn medium-size shirts. There were new suits for graduation, new dresses for recitals and school dances. Church camp, deficiency notices at midterm. Car pools forever, until the kids started driving, then worry.

The boys grew manly and strong, the girls beautiful and smart. Jonathan went through grad school on scholarships. Alan was working at Old Faithful Inn in Yellowstone Park the year of the fires. Jess worried constantly, but he had wonderful stories to tell. Heather got too serious too soon, Jess and Paul thought, but eventually that boyfriend was discarded.

Karl tried to change the visitation schedule, and Jess had to get a lawyer again. Toby started driving. She was belted in, but her face hit the steering wheel when a pickup ran a red light. The plastic surgeon was good, and the scars faded until only Toby and Jess could see them.

Then Toby went through a princess phase that drove Jess crazy and made it a little easier to let her leave for college. She went to school in Laramie, so when Paul got sick she could come home on weekends, just to be there in case Jess needed a break or someone to talk to. All the kids were good when Paul was sick, but a bit self-absorbed as they made their way in the world.

Money was a constant concern. She and Paul earned good salaries, but children and college are expensive. During the first years they were married the price of oil peaked, and they talked about cashing in on the fast money, going to work for an oil company or a land company. Neither one wanted to quit, so they stayed with USGS. As old Wyoming hands knew, after every boom came the bust. Rig permits peaked in December 1981, and after that houses went back to the banks, boomers left for the next boom, and a lot of transplanted ecology emigrants went back East.

Sometimes, when Jess was driving across the sage flats after a rain with the clean smell blowing off the gray-green clumps, or when she was threading her way through the mountains with the pines whispering—a couple of hours with no phone calls, no demands—then Kip would come to mind. Her memories were warm, of love shared, of pain of parting. She needed the open sky and the freedom of being outdoors alone—rounded hills, watered grass, fast creeks. Then, in the quiet she remembered Kip, how he revealed himself. She didn't like all of him, but she treasured the way he shared himself.

She never phoned him or wrote to him except for Christmas cards, to make sure he was still in Lakewood, still somewhere in the world, perhaps thinking of her. He never phoned her, but sent an annual card, address corrected after she remarried.

Jess thought of him when she occasionally read a *Denver Post*, or admired an especially striking sports photo, and she never lost her habit of reading the sideways six-point type next to photos in magazines. Once in a great while, she saw his credit, usually on western wildlife.

When Paul got sick he took early retirement. Jess had always thought leukemia was a disease of young people, but no—it took the older ones, too. The chemo made him sick, and his silver hair fell out and never grew back. They traveled and saw their first grandchild, Alan's Becky in Los Angeles. They visited Jon in grad school in Indiana, and Elisa, just graduating from Cornell, and Heather, working in Chicago while she finished up her degree at Loyola. They were there when Elisa married a computer analyst.

Then they went back to Cheyenne. Jess hated to go to work in the morning, but she knew she couldn't stop the cancer cells' spread, and if she didn't work, she couldn't get through the day.

When she counted the years of her life, she was surprised at how little time she was miserable. A few months after Kip left, a couple of years before and after the divorce, and this last year. Not a bad percentage, out of nearly fifty, but those brief times were so painful, they left scar tissue on her heart.

Paul was so tired and so sick, only cruelty would have kept him alive any longer.

"I want you to live, but not to suffer," Jess had said. He had smiled, tried to talk. He squeezed her hand back. She took him home from the hospital, arranged a leave and hospice workers.

He had been home two weeks when they both awoke early one morning. She asked him if wanted to see the sun come up. When he said yes, she dressed him and pushed his wheelchair out on the deck. They sat together as the last stars faded and the sky grayed with false dawn. When the sun came over the horizon she left him to make breakfast, and when she returned, he was gone. She sat for a long time on the deck and told him good-bye. When she felt calm, she went inside to make arrangements.

The children flew back to attend the funeral. She got to the church early, before the service, and checked flowers and all the things the funeral directors had already checked. She looked into the casket, but it held only the remains—the husk that had been his body. She didn't believe in a heaven with angels playing harps, but she hoped that his spirit was at peace.

Then she sat in the old building that smelled of stone and candles, with the stained glass filtering the sun through color. She wore a royal blue suit with a new pink shell blouse. Tears rolled down her face, and she let them drip onto her bosom. Surely tears wouldn't hurt her new blouse.

Tears were salty water. She knew that pain tears had hormones that chopping-onions tears didn't have. She remembered lying in bed and weeping, tasting the faint ammonia of pain tears—from loss, from shame.

Now, as she sat in the hard pew she blotted her face, hoping that her makeup didn't wash away. There was a long day to be gotten through. She wept again during the service and again at the grave.

At the cemetery she stood on the hemp mat under the canopy and stared at the turned earth. She felt the sun on her face and heard voices.

People would think she was hysterical if she knelt and sank her hands into the rough, dry clods of dirt, but that was what she thought of doing to feel connected by touching the earth. She talked and laughed and wept with the children afterward at home and saw to it that everyone had a place to stay for himself, spouse, or significant other. Heather had a new young man who came back from Chicago with her. Toby watched her mother and led her away when she started shaking.

Jess hung up the royal blue suit and took off the blouse, thinking she could wear it again, but the front was stained from the tears.

Tears should mark silk, she realized. Not only stain, but eat through the fabric. The distilled emotions they carry should burn skin, sear flesh, eat bone, etch glass, melt granite, carve diamonds.

Maybe they did.

Jess lay alone in the big bed. She mourned Paul, but she knew more strongly than she ever had in her life that she was surrounded by children, by friends, by love —by a universe as generous with joy as with tears.

# 19

*When she got off* the tour bus in Glenwood Springs, Jess was stiff from sitting, a little dopey from Dramamine, and short of breath. It was foolish, she thought, but she wanted to travel around the west, and at fifty, she didn't want to drive alone. She wasn't afraid, but she stopped so often it seemed it took forever to get anywhere.

It took her the day's ride from Cheyenne to identify a familiar feeling: she was somewhere west of the one-hundredth meridian, in midsummer, and she remembered how she felt when she first came west—feisty and ambitious and vulnerable. The old hotel looked uncannily familiar. Perhaps she had been here in a previous existence when good things happened to her.

She nodded to one of her seatmates—another widow from her church—and shifted the straps of her tote bag as she got up.

The she walked into the lobby of the Colorado Hotel, a grand oaken-floored anachronism. The room was filled with clusters of white wicker chairs around glass-topped tables. A few couples sipped drinks, looking out the high windows to the gardens growing bright in the cool, high sunlight.

She joined the tour group at the desk where they received room assignments. Most people in the group chose single rooms because they slept poorly. Jess had a new AARP card in her purse. When she was younger she had thought fifty was old—fat, arthritic, sexless. Now that she was here, she didn't feel old, most of the time. And aspirin usually took care of what hurt.

She didn't feel old when she saw herself from a distance in a mirror or shop window—ten pounds over her weight before Toby was born, but rearranged from pregnancy and gains-and-losses. Only when she looked at herself up close in the mirror did she have to acknowledge the silver hair, the wrinkles—all the changes time had made—and then she was surprised that she had gotten this old.

Jess looked forward to the long hours riding through the mountains, looking over the basins and deserts again—a meditation on distances, with landscapes too beautiful to fit into the frame of a movie, slowly changing while the piercing sun arced across empty blue sky.

When she turned toward the elevators she saw a man crossing the lobby. *Couldn't be.* She froze, disbelieving, her heart in her throat. She stood motionless, enjoying that secret pleasure of watching when the subject is unaware. Then she hurried over, longing to hug him, not wanting to frighten him. She touched his arm, and he started as though from an electric current.

"My God, Kip! I never thought I'd see you again."

She brushed away her quick tears. He stared at her and then pulled her into a hard hug. She reached up to stroke the shaggy silver hair.

He said, "Girl, you'll never—" and she felt him gasp in her arms. She breathed him in. Finally, they separated, stepped back to look at each other. He looked shaky, so she pulled him over to one of the chintz-cushioned chairs.

"What are you doing here?" She released his hand to fumble in her bag for a handkerchief, then blew her nose. "Aren't you still in Denver?"

"Just a vacation," he said, then coughed and cleared his throat. "After the funeral."

Jess looked carefully at him and saw the lines around his eyes. "When?"

"End of May."

"You look like you've been stretched thin," she said.

Kip nodded.

Stretched and then some, she thought. What a cold, empty place he must be in now. "I'm sorry. If you want to talk, I'll listen."

"Maybe later." He gave her a phony smile. He looked thinner than ever, with his head bent, shoulders bowed, as though he had been carrying something heavy for a long time, literally.

"You never want to lose them, but they get so bad you can't ask them to stay," Jess said, thinking of Paul and how she had wanted him free of pain. She was happy that his suffering ended but sad that she was without the joy of him.

She reached for Kip's hands again. She wanted to touch him. Maybe she could transfuse some of her vitality. They both had old hands—veins, spots. His hair, now completely silver, looked as though he hadn't seen a barber in months.

"Let's have dinner," she suggested. "You are staying here?"

"Yes. That would be nice." His voice was lifeless, as though he answered only from habit. "I was going to the pool just now, but I'm too tired."

"Let me find my room and change and I'll go with you. You'll feel better if you go."

"I suppose."

They exchanged room numbers and she went to her room, where she quickly dug her least-faded swimsuit and new warm-ups out of her suitcase. She dumped out the contents of her tote and put in shampoo and a few other necessities and an extra towel she had brought. She was concerned about Kip, but she felt lighthearted. It must be the altitude.

In his suite, Kip sat in the overstuffed chair, one leg over the armrest, and looked out the tall, narrow window over the busy resort city. He had given himself a week to stay at this pleasant, impersonal hotel, to rest and think about what to do next. He wanted to get away from the phone and reminders of Megan and the last year. And overly-helpful females. He wanted to escape into silence and see what he found there. Glad as he was to see Jess, he hadn't come here to find her. The wearing cycle of hope, disillusion, revival, and acceptance had exhausted him. He was eligible for early retirement. Why not? He could take on a few photo assignments, go fishing more. He had only worked lately to keep the insurance current, and he'd used up all his leave to spend time with Megan.

He needed to get his feet under him, not get distracted by Jess. He had noticed two Christmases ago when the card read just Jess Storms, not Jess and Paul. He'd sent a note, thought of contacting her then, but Megan was ill and that seemed to absorb all his energy. Each year he seemed to have less.

He didn't know if he could live without Megan. He thought he was prepared, but the utter emptiness stunned him. He thought he knew how hard it would be, but if he had, he couldn't have faced it. It wasn't just her physical presence, it was her caring. As long as she lived, he knew to his depths that she loved him and cared where he was and what he was doing. She died, and he lost that buffer of affection between him and the uncaring world, between him and the demons at his core.

People with asthma can live a long time. But the infections recurred until the doctors at Jewish National couldn't do enough.

Now, a month after the funeral, Jess materialized. He almost winced at her energy, palpable as a motor's hum. Here was life again, and he wasn't ready for it yet. Memories of Jess demanded a hearing, like old vinyl LPs in the attic. Against his will, the murmurs and whispers of old times penetrated his grief.

Wait a minute! he wanted to shout. It's too soon. I'm not ready. I don't know what she wants—but he did know, as he had always known. And he was shocked that he wanted it, too. He should be too numb, too deep in mourning to care or even notice.

She would distract him and see that he ate properly and got some exercise and enough sleep. He remembered in Casper that she had bullied him into taking care of himself. He resented it as he craved it.

He answered her knock, and she swept into the room.

"Come *on*," she said. "I'm going whether you do or not. I can't wait."

Kip thought she looked much as she always had, only softer, older. She must swim all the time to keep those breasts from falling. She had the full shoulders of a swimmer and the defined waist. She was a good-looking middle-aged woman, and too energetic for her own good.

"But I don't feel—" They'd turned up the gravity on him today, and he didn't want Jess to see him seedy.

"Do it anyway," she said softly.

Jess sat down in an overstuffed chair and surveyed Kip's suite, what she could see of it, while he changed. Two double beds in the next room, the living room furniture with an antique armoire hiding the TV. This suite was on the top floor, with a view of the Colorado River, the highway, and the town stretching up the mountain on the other side of the bridge.

She remembered the little room in Thermopolis—threadbare spread, cameras on the dresser, sink in the room. They had gotten more middle-class, older, God, older. But they'd never had more fun.

Kip came out wearing boxer trunks, colors so bright she knew they'd never been worn. She had been wondering how she looked to him. The skin beneath his eyes pouched and his shoulders sagged, but he looked good to her, despite the worst gravity could do.

"Did you know that the ancient people thought springs were sacred?" she said.

He pulled on a baggy set of gray cotton sweats.

"Why was that?" he asked to be polite.

"They thought the gods inside of the earth spoke to humans at springs."

"The earth'd have a hard time getting heard over the public address music and the kids screaming on the water slide down there."

"Still, there's something special, even with city chlorination and concrete decks."

"Do you remember Thermop?" he asked as they walked across the wide hall to the elevator.

"Just now. Did you ever sell any of those pictures you took where the hot water ran into the river?"

"No, but later I made better water pictures. It's like snow—if you don't get the right angle, it looks like a sheet of shiny plastic."

"I didn't see any cameras."

He shrugged.

They strolled across the bridge. She hadn't walked this slowly in years, then she remembered what grief could do. She felt silly and wanted to sing, walk on her hands, turn cartwheels. If this was all they did together—walked over to the pool and had a swim—then it was more than she expected. They separated at the admissions desk at the huge pool. Jess lost several quarters in the locker before she got coordinated and figured it out. She found Kip waiting at the door when she came out. She couldn't keep from beaming each time she saw him, but his expression seemed frozen into that polite half-smile you give the mourners at a funeral.

"Come *on*," she said. But he didn't move. Was he afraid of the hot water? "I'll do CPR if you have a heart attack," she said and laughed. He gave a start, then they left their towels on chairs on the deck and eased into the warmest pool. She remembered those first days when she would get lost thinking about Paul. Megan must still be very alive in his thoughts.

"Oh my, this feels good," she said.

He grunted. They soaked a while, then she left him to go to the cooler end of the pool and swim laps. She was so buoyant because of the minerals that she swam *on* the water, not through it. Swimming laps on vacation smacked of compulsiveness, but it was a healthy habit. She'd worked off loads of frustration, stroking through the water, outdoors in the summer, at the municipal pool in the winter. She had an elaborate routine to protect her white-streaked hair from chlorine.

When she went back Kip was sitting on the edge of the pool with his feet in the water. Another memory came. She picked up his foot and massaged it. He smiled and offered the other. Then they got out and lay on chaises with their towels over their legs.

"Tired?" she asked.

"Devastated. I drove out this morning."

"Tired from the soak, or from everything?"

"By you, girl."

"Go on," she said and they laughed. After a while, she asked: "Have you been ill?"

"No. I have even been running two miles a night, most nights, through it all. It's just that she was sick for so long and took so long to—"

"Say it."

"I didn't want her to die sooner, but it was so hard and she was in pain and—" A flash of anger. "There was nothing I could do."

"I remember. It's been two years and I'm still not used to him being gone."

"Do we ever get used to it?"

"The feelings change, but they don't go away. At first it's like being hit with a wrecking ball three or four times a day."

She looked at his bleak face. "Are you ready to go back?" She wondered if he could make the uphill grade to the hotel. He looked gray.

* * *

"Traveling alone?" he asked. He teased the creamy white fish off the bone. The pleasant din of china and silver filled the dining room.

"With a tour group." Jess forked green beans.

"You were driving alone when we first met. I thought you were awfully brave and gutsy." He looked across the table and smiled. "Still do."

"Thanks." She cut a bite of steak. "With a little help from my friends." She remembered hard home truths and murmured comfort he'd given her at Chico.

He wore a laundry-starched shirt, a sober tie, and a charcoal suit. She didn't think she'd ever seen him this dressed up. More middle class signs. She was glad she'd worn the best dress she had packed—a silky turquoise shirt dress with a heavy pueblo Indian silver necklace. Silver hair, silver jewelry. She hadn't even packed heels, but wore comfortable SAS sandals.

"How come you're here?" he asked, and again she saw the polite half smile.

"Driving alone has gotten harder and harder. I've driven hundreds of thousands of miles, mostly in Wyoming, usually in a pickup. I thought being driven would be a treat."

"Is it?" He poked at a potato, then put his fork down, leaving it only half eaten.

"Partly. Not as much freedom, but consequently little responsibility. I just 'go along with'—whatever is planned. We're not pushing very hard."

"You were lively earlier. At the pool." He sipped a glass of Riesling.

"Had to get the kinks out. I'll sleep tonight."

There was a silence while she worked on her steak.

Kip went away and when he came back he said, "I wish I could sleep."

"It takes a while. Recovery time. This is a good place."

"How long does your tour stay here?" he asked.

"A couple of days. Why don't you come to the vapor caves with us tomorrow? There's room on the bus."

"I don't think so."

"Doc Holliday came to Glenwood for the vapors," she said.

"He died anyway."

# 20

*After dinner they strolled* around perfect, weedless gardens. High-altitude flowers always seemed brighter, their colors clearer. Jess had deep pink roses in her yard in Cheyenne that sometimes bloomed late into the fall, sheltered by the house, November roses. No perfume, but hardy enough to survive the first frosts. She always wanted them to last till Christmas.

"Shall I see you to your door?" he asked. They stood at the elevators. He ran a finger around his collar, then slid his hand inside his coat to scratch his ribs.

"No, I'm fine," she said. "What's wrong?"

"Itchy."

"Didn't you shower when we got back?"

"Of course. Dry skin."

"I've got some lotion."

"Don't fuss."

She phoned his room the next morning and urged him to join her group. He went along with them, but without much interest.

"If you let me, I'll boss you around," she said, half-kidding. "I remember feeling relieved when decisions were made for me, right after Paul died. Besides, I'm a supervisor—I'm used to telling people what to do."

Kip didn't know if he wanted that or not.

After lunch, he said he needed a nap, so she said she'd pick him up to go to the pool at four. He went back to his room and stared at the ceiling for a while. He hadn't thought it possible to live so long on four or five hours of sleep a night, but he had, for years now. He didn't want a nap, he wanted silence. Jess's talking exhausted him. It seemed foreign to talk about himself.

After a while he got up and went into the bathroom. He stripped and looked at himself in the full-length mirror. God, how had he gotten so stooped over? He straightened up and found it hard to pull stiff shoulders straight. He hadn't run for a week. Maybe today he'd swim laps too.

He took aspirin and put his trunks on and picked up the Lawrence Block mystery from his nightstand.

When Jess came, she handed him a bottle of dry skin lotion.

"I'll put sunscreen on," he said and handed it back.

They swam, went back to the hotel, and decided to drive into town for dinner. Afterward he saw her to the elevator.

"When is your tour leaving?" he asked.

"Tomorrow." She looked down. "I'd like to stay another day or so with you, but only if you want me to."

"How will you get home?"

"I can always rent a car."

"You'll lose your money."

"That's not the point. I feel like I found a good luck charm I thought I'd lost."

"Stay."

• • •

They met at breakfast. They sat at the same table in companionable silence. Jess never spoke until she ate a hefty breakfast and drank stout coffee. He never talked, either, at breakfast.

"Do you ever wonder what would have happened if we had stayed together?" she asked, after a second cup of coffee, granola, yogurt, English muffin, juice.

"If you had come to New York with me?" He finished oatmeal and the last corner of toast.

"Yes. How our lives would have been different?"

"I did think of it, a long time ago. Irresistible," he said. "But it always came out—" He grinned. "A disaster."

"You know, I think you're right. We were different people then. I was selfish, or self-absorbed. I thought I knew what I wanted. And how to get it. By myself."

"I was flying on ambition. Nothing I wouldn't try."

"We probably would have had a couple of good years," said Jess, imagining her twenty-five-year-old self in that alternate life. "I would have tried to be a good little wifey and gone nuts living in a city. Trying to make like Mrs. Cleaver, with my Midwestern values." She laughed.

"I was gone a lot," Kip said. "It was wild—Woodstock and everybody doing drugs. I always hear The Doors in my head when I think of that time."

"We would have shaken apart," Jess said. "I wasn't even ready to get married when I married Karl, but the biological imperative was working. As bad as that time was, I wouldn't want to change it—I got Toby."

"How is she?" Kip asked, breaking the mood.

"Great. She's beautiful. She's almost through with college. I wanted her to go out of state, but with all the other kids scattered around the country, I'm glad she's in Laramie. She is studying to be a wildlife biologist."

She moved into his suite and slept in the other bed. They swam in the morning, before the tourists thronged the huge mineral pool. She planned outings to "places of interest." He drove his Bronco, and she navigated. Looking like tourists in their pastel sweatshirts and cotton slacks, they visited Doc Holliday's disputed grave. They drove to Aspen for a concert. They drove to Leadville and traipsed around the Victorian buildings .

They went to a supermarket in Glenwood and put together a picnic lunch, which they took to a nearby national forest. They sat at the official government picnic table and assembled sandwiches. They had bottled fruit juice and a six-pack of beer, but no chips or cookies—a low-cholesterol picnic. They scurried to the Bronco when the afternoon rain shot silver through sunlight.

"Tell me about Megan," said Jess. The storm pelted the car, and the windows steamed over.

"It's too fresh," said Kip.

"I don't want to push you. But if you do want to talk, I'm here, and I went through something similar two years ago. And the funeral was just the end. He had been sick for a year, that we knew of, and I was worn out from a year of watching him die." Jess wiped her tears and took a pull on her beer.

Kip leaned across the seat and patted her arm. They sat in the car and the light changed through the Impressionist blur of rain on the windshield as the storm blew past.

"It started a long time ago," Kip said. "When did I see you last?"

"August of—" Jess counted on her fingers. "Seventy-eight. Twelve years to June 1990, today."

"It started before that, before Aquilino left Denver. It happened so gradually—after a while those trips to the hospital with her gasping beside me seemed—usual. I always remember one about a year after I saw you. It was toward the end of the school year, which is always crazy, and Aquilino was preparing for a recital and a couple of auditions. She was working too hard. She crashed, and I thought it was just stress, which she had plenty of just then.

"It was a close call—she had to cancel summer classes. She went back to teaching that fall semester. Later, when I was going through doctor bills for taxes, I could see the episodes were coming more often.

"She fought it," he continued. He looked at Jess's profile, then into the rain-sheeted windshield and saw the past.

"She had one of the best asthma specialists in the country, and she followed orders, exercised as much as she could, took her treatments, took her medicine—she was doing her part.

"I would have been so depressed," said Kip. "I wouldn't have gotten out of bed if it had been me. But she pushed herself to keep moving, tried to be cheerful for my sake."

"Did you give up sex?" Jess asked.

"Not for a long time, probably longer than Megan enjoyed it. I wanted her to know she was loved. She did fine as long as she could sit up and breathe. I didn't know how inventive I could be until then." He tried to hide a small smile.

"You'll have to explain that some time."

Kip rolled down the car window. The fresh smell after the rain was better than perfume. Jess rolled her window down too.

"One day, when she'd had a rough bout, Megan seemed frightened for the first time. Or for the first time she let me know she was frightened.

"'I can't go to the hospital again,' she said. And I asked, 'Why not?' I remember we were listening to the "Trout Quintet" on the speakers she had wired in the bedroom.

"'Kip, I'm afraid,'" she said. 'All the medicine isn't working. The infection isn't clearing up. They have discussed aggressive treatment. I'm tired. I don't want aggressively to fight to stay alive like this.'

"And I said, 'I can't do without you,' making a joke of it. 'You'll just have to fight.'

"'Really, I can't do this,' she whispered. And I knew then that she would die. Because she realized what the doctors would not admit: they couldn't win this one.

"'Don't let them keep doing things to me, please,' she begged. I couldn't talk, so I nodded and promised. She talked calmly and rationally and said that she was having periods when she couldn't remember things and she wanted me to know now what she wanted. She said, 'I want you to know that I love you. I am thankful every day I live that we married. You've given me enough love to keep ten women alive, if love could do that.' "

Kip's face convulsed, that sudden, hard contraction of pain that only happened a few times. Tears filled his eyes. He turned away from Jess, rested his head on the steering wheel until he could talk.

He shook his head to clear away the memory, and said to Jess: "I've heard of people willing themselves to die. I think she did that. Her lungs and heart just quit. Aquilino and I cried in each other's arms at the funeral.

"Something funny happened I never told anybody. It's crazy, but it's true. I was sleeping in the guest bedroom and I heard a noise or something that woke me. I walked down the hall. It was silent in the room. I reached over to touch her hand. It was cold. I looked, and she wasn't breathing, but I felt her still there. I took her earphones off and I heard Bach, faint piano ripples. I thought I saw something and looked out the window. She was there, saying good-bye. She was happy. I whispered good-bye, and she faded into the stars."

Each night after dinner, Kip and Jess went back to his suite and Jess rubbed light mineral oil—baby oil without the perfume—into his skin. It was a way to communicate caring without words. For Jess this dream state lasted four or five days. She didn't think, didn't plan more than one day at a time, didn't acknowledge any feelings or desires of her own. She floated, a body in the swimming pool, pushed by the currents other swimmers created.

Tonight he lay on his stomach. She rubbed oil into the grainy texture of his back. Except for his face, neck and arms, he was pale, with age markers and veins visible. She worked her fingers into the fissures in his neck, kneaded the stiff ligaments. Then she softly pushed the knotted muscles of his shoulders, pushed against his resistance until he relaxed. She worked her way down the vertebrae, a thumb and forefinger counting each hollow beside the spine. He was still hard-muscled under his loose puppy skin.

She lost herself, thinking of sensations when her back was rubbed—she was as much touched as touching.

She hadn't let herself know what she felt until he said, "Do you want to make love?"

She kept rubbing a hairy calf, a hard runner's calf.

"No. I don't give charity fucks. Or take them," she said. "You need something else, not sex."

"You don't want to?"

"I didn't say that." Because now that he made her think about it, she was turned on. Ten minutes with Kip and she felt her body soften, warm, dampen, relax. She had been floating on a raft of arousal since the first day. She wondered, after two years-plus of living without sex, if she still lubricated.

"It's too soon for you," she said, finishing up with that foot and starting the other leg.

"I feel ten years younger than I did when I came here. I've been half asleep for a long time—when Megan was sick, before she died."

Jess poked her fingers around the kneecap, then massaged the other calf. "You look better." She smoothed his ankle tendons with an oily thumb. "Except for your hair."

"Oh, yes. I need a haircut." Kip rolled over on his back. She picked up the oil and dribbled a stream onto his chest. She sat beside him on the bed, working impersonally as a nurse, pulling and pushing. She smoothed more oil over his belly and noticed he was erect.

"It's got a mind of it's own," he said.

She remembered a coupling when they were young—so sweet and fast she was dizzy. She wanted to jump on him now. She *thought* she wanted to. But there was just so much that had happened to them both. She was afraid she couldn't keep him erect or that she couldn't respond or that memories would interfere.

"Come here," he said. He sat up and held out an arm. She sat beside him. He gave her a buddy squeeze. "Who decides what I need?"

"Sorry. I'm very good at bossing people around."

# 21

*They sat side by side* on the bed, leaning against the headboard.

"I'm not sure what I want, or what you want," she said.

"I came here to Glenwood to think. Instead, I've been running around, having a good time with you."

"Maybe that's what you needed. I know it's been great just finding you again. I don't know if I want more." Jess smoothed her shirt. "We aren't the same people we were."

"We're them and three or four others besides."

"And we don't know each other, Kip. We know our memories, what we shared—but not all the rest. I don't know much about your time with Megan. You don't know about me and Paul. Or the kids. Maybe we're just being nostalgic and this can't work over the long haul."

"And you're being practical and reasonable, trying to consider all the contingencies."

"Of course."

In a low conspiratorial voice he said: "No guarantees.

You know that." He shifted and pulled her closer. She pushed a pillow between the headboard and the small of her back.

"We can work out in advance as many details as we can think of," she said. "Who lives where, who uses the downstairs medicine cabinet. Who is on whose medical insurance. One thing for sure—we've got to be able to talk like this so we *can* work things out. And say what we feel."

He squeezed her shoulder and said: "And the other guy has to listen. We know we can't think of everything. Things will happen that we didn't plan for." He saw her expression become grave. "Paul?"

She nodded.

"It doesn't quit hurting?"

"You just get used to it. Oh Kip." She turned her face into his shoulder and wept for a moment.

Kip knew that when grief scars you never get used to it.

"Feeling good isn't disloyalty to Paul," he said, and she cried harder. "Other things you never planned," he said. "Good things. Five kids, all turning out okay. Your health, so you can travel."

"Finding you again." Jess wiped her face with the sheet.

"Have you worked out all the variables to your satisfaction?"

"No. Tell me what you're going to do."

"I don't want to go back to Lakewood. Too many memories. But I have to. At least long enough to move out. I don't want to go back to the newspaper. I can retire early. I think I'll do that."

"Then what?" asked Jess. She wasn't ready to retire, not with Toby still in school.

"Then I show up on your doorstep again."

She looked at him, and he was grinning. She saw the young Kip, full of energy, and the burnt-out Kip, and the thoughtful Kip who could love her and send her on her way. Like a vision, she could see him as an old, old man. Smiling, smiling.

This didn't seem real. There had been times when she wanted Kip—funny and bright and unpredictable and energetic. This was usually when her life wasn't going well and the idea of Kip was an escape. She had written letters to him that she hadn't mailed. Now it was happening. She needed to work off this tension.

"I'm going to cut your hair," Jess said. She bounded off the bed and got a towel from the bathroom. "Sit here," she said, indicating a straight chair. She rummaged through her tote for scissors.

"What kind of answer is that?" he growled, getting up slowly. He pulled on his boxers.

"No answer. I can't think straight."

"Should I let you have the scissors?"

Jess ran her hand through his hair. It was thinner, silver, as soft as ever. She remembered cutting his hair when it was as black as ebony. She snipped slowly, carefully, so it wouldn't look amateurish. As long as she could touch or see or taste or hear something tangible, she was all right. "If you retire, you still have to go back and finish up the paperwork, don't you? You can't just walk away."

"Yes. In fact, I will probably stay on a couple of months, to get everything worked out. I haven't seriously gone over the offer."

"Will you have enough to live on?"

"I don't know."

"You don't know!" Jess stopped snipping.

"I assume so. I can always pick up free-lance assignments, or even teach a class or two."

"I could support us. Or I might even retire. Then we really wouldn't have enough money."

"Enough for what?"

"Bills, emergencies, medical."

"I don't even know what I owe the hospital."

"Kip! You've got to take care of business. I know, I know, you've been doing it all for a long time. But there're a few more things to do."

"I don't want to do them. And the other hard jobs—going through Megan's things."

"Don't. Let her friends do it. Surely she had women friends."

"Dozens. That's a good idea, but do you realize how many casseroles I will have to eat?"

Jess laughed and blew cut hairs off Kip's neck. "The widower's brigade," she said.

"Here, I haven't even asked you properly," said Kip.

"Don't! You'll never get up." Jess laughed. This made her nervous.

He knelt in front of her, the bath towel still around his neck like some tacky cape trimmed with silver hair. "Will you?" His smile was powerfully persuasive.

"I've never said no to you."

"Good." He got up and sat in the chair again.

"I just have some misgivings—" Jess said. "What if, well, physically it doesn't work?" She snipped.

"We can check that out any time you like," Kip said with a devilish expression.

"The first time we were young and ambitious. Work stood in the way," she said. "The second time I was married, had Karl, had the baby. The last time you had Megan and I needed to get my head together." She evened up a place over his ears, then brushed him off with the towel. "One thing—this time there's nothing in the way." She stopped because she was cold. "I'm scared."

"Nothing to stop us, if we have enough nerve," he said. Jess felt giddy, as though the floor were tipping. She groped for him, wrapped her arms around him. Longing surged through her like fever and she thought she might faint if she couldn't hold on.

"Every time I saw you I still loved you," he said. "Something—the universe or circumstances or fate—brought us together three times by chance—the Valverde Hotel, La Fonda, and here in Glenwood. That defies the laws of chance, doesn't it? We can't expect the universe to keep doing this indefinitely."

"I guess not."

"We've both had the bad parts so recently, we're afraid to let the good parts happen," he said. "We don't know if we could stay together. We never tried. I don't know nothin' 'bout birthin' no babies, Miz Scarlett. But we did it anyway."

Jess smiled.

"Do you remember," he said, "a long time ago, in Santa Fe? I said if our bodies remember pain and hurt, they remember love?" Kip was talking faster now. It was as though he talked energy into existence, as though he were recreating the person he had been before grief drained him.

"Yes. I was nursing Toby. I've thought of that many times. That's why I wanted to rub your back—to give you something to store. When we're skin hungry we forget what it feels like to be touched."

"People like us, who have lived lives with other people—we bring all the people we've known—the spouses, the lovers, your children."

"And grandchild. One so far."

"And so we aren't just two people. We've stored each other from years ago and we've stored all these other people who loved us. And we bring them all with us."

"I never thought of it that way," said Jess. Her emotions suddenly triggered a hot flash, despite the hormones, the little yellow pill that kept the fire demon quiet. She blotted her face with her sleeve.

"Think of it this way: there is no end of the love we have been given," he said.

She wasn't arguing with Kip, but he seemed to need to persuade her, to persuade himself. "It's still here," he said, "in the cells and blood, muscles, guts, and bones. In murmurs of the heart, in touches, in words. We hold all the good things that happened to us."

Jess nodded, too touched to speak.

"You've been loved, so you could love me, give what you thought I needed."He paced back and forth a couple of laps, then said abruptly, "I'll give you a few minutes to yourself. I need some razors and Gaviscon. Can I get you anything from K-Mart before they close?" She said no and he quickly dressed.

He kissed her absently as he went out the door. Only when he stood in front of the elevators did he realize what he had done. He had taken her for granted with that automatic gesture. It felt right.

Kip felt the beginnings of a rejuvenating process that would hurt, like growing pains, but would bring him back to life.

Flashbacks came—images without words. The woman at the Valverde Hotel. He'd never seen a baby born.

Jess in her little apartment in Casper—jeans and no makeup and her face glowing. Slowly, the words came back: "I missed you more than I missed sleep."

The cathedral in Santa Fe with the one warm spot for the Virgin. "That's not how I feed her."

He remembered noises Jess made when they made love, from hums and sighs to shrieks of delight. The troubled woman floating, hair fanned in the water, Montana sky over the Chico pool: "I've messed up so badly."

And he heard himself: "Here, stop that when I'm lecturing," as they lay on the snow raft with the telescope.

Beatles songs and Byrds, Jefferson Airplane.

He found his car, got in, missed the K-Mart the first time by.

The memories in his head, images always and murmurs of the heart, of things they had said: "Everybody needs to be somebody's something." He'd been rough on her that day.

He heard those small sounds remembered from showers together and dinner dishes washed and the light through the bedroom window, the wind outside. He listened to his own heart, heard the murmurs there and knew this would be the right thing. He heard music, he didn't remember what piece it was, but the melody soared—lovely and boundless and optimistic—and reached where words couldn't go.

Jess sat with her feet up and stared out the window as the light faded. This was when she missed Paul the most—the quiet time after dinner, in high summer when the dark blue sky began to shimmer with stars. She had a million doubts: practical considerations of money and compatibility. How much of what they assumed about each other would be true? She really thought they'd be okay in bed. Hadn't they always? But life is lived away from the lover's field.

Kip returned and dropped a plastic bag on the table. A red plastic bottle stuck out.

He came over and took one hand and pulled her to her feet. "Shall we try it?"

"Only way to find out," she said. She couldn't swallow.

He kissed her tentatively, softly.

Jess took a deep breath and felt herself lean into him. She wrapped her arms around him. "What if it doesn't work?"

"At least we can say we tried." Kip kissed her neck and she shivered.

"I think I remember the next part," Jess said. She took his face in her hand and brought him into a long kiss.

"We are absurd," said Kip. She could feel a laugh begin in his belly.

Jess laughed. "We are. Two old folks like us."

"We're not old!"

"Old is okay. Old is good. But we're not supposed to feel like this."

"Or act like this." Kip ran his hands under her shirt, found her taut nipples. She unbuttoned his shirt. They reached for each other again. There was no hurry. They had waited a long time. Kip murmured soft love words. Jess sighed. She was a fountain of anticipation, filling with pleasure. Kip breathed faster, and she felt him erect against her belly.

"What's in the sack?" she asked.

"Soap bubbles," he said. "For after."

## AVAILABLE NOW

### A SEASON OF ANGELS by Debbie Macomber

From bestselling author Debbie Macomber comes a heartwarming and joyful story of three angels named Mercy, Goodness, and Shirley who must grant three prayers before Christmas. "*A Season of Angels* is charming and touching in turns. It would take a real Scrooge not to enjoy this story of three ditsy angels and answered prayers."—Elizabeth Lowell, bestselling author of *Untamed.*

### MY FIRST DUCHESS by Susan Sizemore

Jamie Scott was an impoverished nobleman by day and a masked highwayman by night. With four sisters, a grandmother, and one dowager mother to support, Jamie seized the chance to marry a headstrong duchess with a full purse. Their marriage was one of convenience, until Jamie realized that he had fallen hopelessly in love with his wife. A delightful romp from the author of the award-winning *Wings of the Storm.*

### PROMISE ME TOMORROW by Catriona Flynt

Norah Kelly was determined to make a new life for herself as a seamstress in Arizona Territory. When persistent cowboys came courting, Norah's five feet of copper-haired spunk and charm needed some protection. Sheriff Morgan Treyhan offered to marry her, if only to give them both some peace . . . until love stole upon them.

### A BAD GIRL'S MONEY by Paula Paul

Alexis Runnels, the black sheep of a wealthy Texas family, joins forces with her father's business rival and finds a passion she doesn't bargain for. A heartrending tale from award-winning author Paula Paul that continues the saga begun in *Sweet Ivy's Gold.*

### THE HEART REMEMBERS by Lenore Carroll

The first time Jess and Kip meet is in the 1960s at an Indian reservation in New Mexico. The chemistry is right, but the timing is wrong. Not until twenty-five years later do they realize what their hearts have known all along. A moving story of friendships, memories, and love.

### TO LOVE AND TO CHERISH by Anne Hodgson

Dr. John Fauxley, the Earl of Manseth, vowed to protect Brianda Breedon at all costs. She didn't want a protector, but a man who would love and cherish her forever. From the rolling hills of the English countryside, to the glamorous drawing rooms of London, to the tranquil Scottish lochs, a sweeping historical romance that will send hearts soaring.

## COMING NEXT MONTH

### DREAM KEEPER by Parris Afton Bonds

The spellbinding Australian saga begun with *Dream Time* continues with the lives and loves of estranged twins and their children, who were destined to one day fulfill the Dream Time legacy. An unforgettable love story.

### DIAMOND IN THE ROUGH by Millie Criswell

Brock Peters was a drifter—a man with no ties and no possessions other than his horse and gun. He didn't like entanglements, didn't like getting involved, until he met the meanest spinster in Colorado, Prudence Daniels. "Poignant, humorous, and heartwarming."—*Romantic Times*

### LADY ADVENTURESS by Helen Archery

A delightful Regency by the author of *The Season of Loving*. In need of money, Stara Carltons resorted to pretending to be the notorious highwayman, One-Jewel Jack, and held up the coach containing Lady Gwendolen and Marcus Justus. Her ruse was successful for a time until Marcus learned who Stara really was and decided to turn the tables on her.

### PRELUDE TO HEAVEN by Laura Lee Guhrke

A passionate and tender historical romance of true love between a fragile English beauty and a handsome, reclusive French painter. "Brilliant debut novel! Laura Lee Guhrke has written a classic love story that will touch your heart."—Robin Lee Hatcher

### PRAIRIE LIGHT by Margaret Carroll

Growing up as the adopted daughter of a prominent Boston family, Kat Norton always knew she must eventually come face-to-face with her destiny. When she travels to the wilds of Montana, she discovers her Native American roots and the love of one man who has always denied his own roots.

### A TIME TO LOVE by Kathleen Bryant

A heartwarming story of a man and woman driven apart by grief who reunite years later to learn that love can survive anything. Eighteen years before, a family tragedy ended a budding romance between Christian Foster and his best friend's younger sister, Willa. Now a grown woman, Willa returns to the family island resort in Minnesota to say good-bye to the past once and for all, only to discover that Christian doesn't intend to let her go.

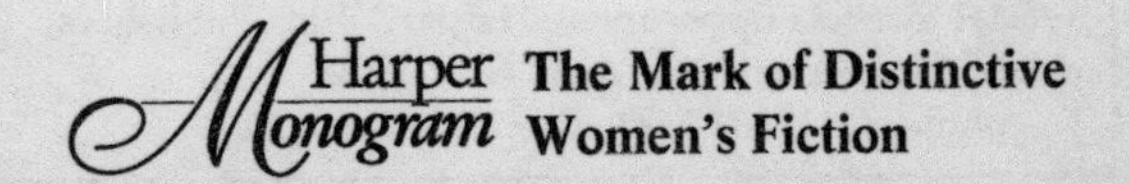